"A chilling story well told. The pace never slows in this noir thriller, taking readers on a stark trail of fear."
CAROLYN G. HART, N.Y. Times and USA Today Bestselling Author

"I love the way this man writes! I adore his style. There is something about it that makes me feel as if I'm someplace I'm not supposed to be, seeing things I'm not supposed to see and that is so delicious."
REBECCA FORESTER, USA Today Bestselling Author

This book "is creative and captivating. It features bold characters, witty dialogue, exotic locations, and non-stop action. The pacing is spot-on, a solid combination of intrigue, suspense, and eroticism. A first-rate thriller, this book is damnably hard to put down. It's a tremendous read."
FOREWORD REVIEWS

"A terrifying, gripping cross between James Patterson and John Grisham. Hansen has created a truly killer thriller."
J.A. KONRATH, USA Today and Amazon Bestselling Author

"As engaging as the debut, this exciting blend of police procedural and legal thriller recalls the early works of Scott Turow and Lisa Scottoline."
LIBRARY JOURNAL

"The well-crafted storyline makes this a worthwhile read. Stuffed with gratuitous sex and over-the-top violence, this novel has a riveting plot."
KIRKUS REVIEWS

"Verdict: The pacing is relentless in this debut, a hard-boiled novel with a shocking ending. The supershort chapters will please those who enjoy a James Patterson–style page-turner"

ISLAND WOMAN

THRILLER PUBLISHING GROUP, INC.

ISLAND WOMAN

**JIM MICHAEL HANSEN
R.J. JAGGER**

THRILLER PUBLISHING GROUP, INC.

ISLAND WOMAN

Thriller Publishing Group, Inc.

Copyright©JimMichaelHansen

Library of Congress Control Number: Available

ISBN 978-1-954518-50-6

For Eileen

1

Four Months Before it all Began
Port-au-Prince, Haiti
February, Karnaval

Twilight washed over Haiti with an evil beat, cloaking Port-au-Prince in ever-deepening shadows and drumming the streets and sins and sounds and smells and gyrations of Karnaval to an even edgier level. In another half hour it would be full dark and that was fine with Kovi-Ke. That's when the senses sharpened, the men went on the hunt and the women got wicked. That's when things that shouldn't happen did.

That's when life became alive.

Dancers, music, floats, hands in the air, bodies shaking, smiles too big for faces, brains on fire, hormones over the edge, an out-of-control bonfire attitude—that's what Karnaval was. It would go on until every wanton soul got its fill and the whole crazy thing imploded of its own exhaustion on Fat Tuesday.

Although she was born and raised and lived in Jamaica a mere puddle jump away, this was Kovi-Ke's first encounter with it, in fact her first visit to Haiti. Twenty-seven, with a friendly smile and a strong body toned by sand sprinting and coral diving, she was well equipped to take advantage of everything it had to offer.

Right now she was solo.

Tomorrow Rea would fly in and then the party would start in earnest.

She bought a bottle of water from a street vender and twisted through the crowd deeper into the guts of the city, looking for a bar or club where she could sit down and see who approached her. If the right man did, well, that would be fine; or the right woman.

Life was for living.

The bodies were thick around her, hot and sweaty and full of energy. Pot hung in the air. Hands held red solo cups, filled with beer or wine or rum or whatever. Several blocks up ahead a group belted out Reggae on a large stage of flashing lights and thundering bass. They must be good because the crowd was jammed in for blocks.

She headed that way.

Halfway there something happened she didn't expect.

Her brain clouded.

Her feet wobbled.

She was on the verge of collapse.

Suddenly a man was by her side, a strong man with a heavily tattooed right arm, a rugged face and long black dreadlocks.

"Pretty lady, are you okay?"

Before she could say, "Yes," her legs collapsed.

The man caught her before she hit the ground.

Then everything turned black.

DAY ONE

(Four Months Later)
June 4
Wednesday

2

June 4
Wednesday Evening

In his garage after dark Wednesday night, Nick Teffinger, the 34-year-old head of Denver's homicide department, did one of his favorite things in the world, namely sat behind the wheel of the '67 and stared through the windshield as a wicked storm ripped the sky with lightning and did its best to tear the world apart. It was a good scene, an ancient one. Dinosaurs had seen it, so had pharaohs and gladiators and the little birds that fought for breadcrumbs down on the 16th Street Mall, that were right now huddled wherever it was that they went to at a time like this.

Two Buds were in his gut and a third was in his hand.

He lived on the side of Green Mountain up near the top where the asphalt stopped, third house from the end. Traffic was minimal so it was unusual when headlights punched up the street through the weather. It was even more unusual when they pulled in front of his house and went out.

The driver got out, hunched against the weather and trotted up the driveway for the front door.

It was a woman, a black woman.

Teffinger shouted, "I'm in here."

She entered the garage, saw where he was and said, "Are you Nick Teffinger?"

The words were broken English, Jamaican maybe.

"Yes."

"My name's Kovi-Ke Gray," she said. "I want to talk to you about something."

"Sure. Do I know you?"

"No."

She hopped in and came into better focus. Her face was nice, her body was strong; down below were simple jeans and up top was a white T, a short one that let her bellybutton show.

"You want some wine or a beer?"

"No. Do you mind if I smoke though?"

He shrugged.

"Go for it."

She lit up, not a cigarette, a joint, taking a deep drag, holding it in and then passing it to him. He hesitated, then took it and did the same.

"A man's in Denver," she said.

"Who?"

"I don't know his name but he's going to kill someone named Station Smith," she said. "I warned her but she thought I was crazy."

"Why?"

"Because the way I know, I can see through his eyes."

"I don't follow."

"I get flashes," she said. "It's like I'm him, looking out of his eyes. I see what he sees. What I saw was him stalking her."

Teffinger shook his head.

"Lady, you're pretty, I'll give you that—"

"I don't expect you to believe me," she said. "Even I don't believe me. What's happening isn't possible. There's no explanation for it. All I can tell you is it's true."

Teffinger frowned.

"Nothing like that can happen," he said.

"I know," she said. "Station Smith, she works at Channel 8." She took another drag, passed the joint to Teffinger and got out. "I'm staying at the Sheraton downtown."

Then she was gone.

DAY TWO

June 5
Thursday

3

June 5
Thursday Morning

Teffinger woke before the sun Thursday morning, threw on sweats and headed out into the crisp dark air for a three-mile run. The exotic little beauty, Kovi-Ke, ricocheted inside his skull as the streetlights clicked off and the neighborhood dogs barked their little warnings. What she said wasn't true. No one could see out of another person's eyes. So, why was her pretty little kissable mouth claiming she could?

What was her game?

Whatever it was, it came in a nice package; a package he wouldn't mind unwrapping. He could spend a week in a secluded lagoon with her, no problem; get rum in his gut and put the world on hold, hell, throw it away for that matter—never come back.

The Sheraton.

He'd find himself down there at some point today for some reason, even if he had to make one up; he already knew that. First though, he wanted to talk to Station Smith, the supposed target, arguably to be sure nothing weird was going on in her life, but just as equally because it was an opportunity to meet her. Half of the male population of Denver had a crush on her. In his honest moments, which luckily weren't many, Teffinger would have to admit he was a part of that group. Station Smith came onto the scene two years ago as the Channel 8 weather announcer and, since that day, storms had never looked so good.

A phone call and explanation got him an appointment with her mid-morning at the TV station, in a large lobby area overlooking Civic Park, replete with coffee. Abstract art hung on the wall, looking like a car had slammed into it at a freaky speed. The woman turned out to be a good size, five-eight or thereabouts to Teffinger's six-two. With no makeup and slightly ruffled hair she looked like health itself, a surfer girl maybe, the kind that got the Beach Boys all riled up and made them write songs.

"Your eyes are two different colors," Station said.

He nodded.

"Either the blue one's supposed to be green or the green one's supposed to be blue," he said. "I've never figured out which. Tell me about the Jamaican woman."

Her face grew serious.

"Am I in danger?"

"You tell me."

"No."

"Does anyone have a reason to kill you?"

"No. You can't be taking any of this seriously."

"Even a little?"

She tightened her brow. "I get emails, we all do. Some of them get a little weird. The really strange ones we run down just to be sure a real life boogieman isn't on the other side.

That doesn't happen often and nothing too serious has ever taken shape."

"Has anyone been following you around?"

"No."

"Do you have a boyfriend?"

"No." She took a sip of coffee, stared over the edge and said, "Send your application in."

He smiled.

"Can I get better weather that way?"

"Not on the first date."

He smiled.

The more she talked, the less Teffinger found anything to be worried about. No crazies were in her life, she hadn't witnessed a murder or come across sensitive information, she didn't owe anyone money, she didn't do drugs, she didn't know the Jamaican woman prior to being approached yesterday, she didn't have a dungeon in her basement, or even a basement for that matter; she was just a surfer girl living a surfer life under a sky full of rays.

He handed her his business card and said, "If you see anyone following you, call me. If you see the Jamaican woman again, call me. Deal?"

"Deal."

"I'm going to go back to the office now and start working on that application."

She handed him her card.

"That's my cell number. Call me when it's done."

4

June 5
Thursday Morning

Outside, the Denver sun went straight to Teffinger's brain and put a spring in his step. Station was interested in him, at least to the point of initial curiosity. She could end up being a big part of his life if he wanted her badly enough and made a serious play for her. She made sense on almost every level and was built of long-term material. He could make little Teffs and be a happy guy. Still, when he closed his eyes, the deep nasty part of his brain gyrated to Kovi-Ke. He kept getting an image of slamming her against the wall and taking her like the devil himself.

Why?

He needed to kill that thought.

The woman made no sense, not on any level other than physical, not to mention that she was deep adrift in some kind of dark game.

Suddenly something happened he didn't expect. He spotted the woman; a distance away and cloaked behind oversized sunglasses, a baseball cap and baggy clothes, but it was her. He already knew the body and the posture and the way she tilted her head slightly to the left.

He headed that way.

His heart raced.

"Are you waiting for Station to come out?"

"Yes."

"Why, do you have something else to tell her?"

"No. I want to see who follows her."

"And then what?"

"Then I'll know whose eyes I'm seeing through."

Teffinger shifted his feet.

"Tell me about that, how you see through his eyes."

"I thought you don't believe me."

"I don't but tell me anyway," he said. "Maybe I'll change my mind."

She studied him and saw it there in his eyes, the fact that he'd never change his mind. She also saw that he wasn't patronizing her. He really did want to hear what was going on with her.

"I get flashes," she said. "They're there in my brain all of a sudden, sort of like in a peripheral way. It's not like I suddenly stop seeing through my own eyes. I don't. They're more like a thought and the more I concentrate on them the clearer they get."

"How long do they last?"

She shrugged.

"Ten seconds up to a minute or two; never very long."

"How often do you get them?"

"There's no pattern," she said. "I've had as many as a dozen in a week and other times nothing for weeks on end."

"Are they in real time?"

"I don't know for sure. I think some are in real time or

close to real time and others aren't. Let me give you an example. On Saturday he came into my head. He was driving a car. It was twilight and the sun was in front of him, meaning he was heading west. He was on a freeway but the traffic was minimal."

"What else?"

"He was listening to the radio."

"What kind of music?"

"Some kind of alternative thing. Have you ever heard The Cure?"

Teffinger shrugged.

"Friday I'm in Love."

"Yeah, I know that song. It was something like them."

"Was it them?"

"It could have been. The point is that he came into my head on Saturday evening driving a car, heading west. The next time he came into my head was a little before noon on Monday. He was following a woman; stalking her, there was no doubt. She was a blond wearing a white skirt and a white blouse and carrying a yellow purse. She was headed for a large building that said TV 8 near the entrance."

"Where she works."

She nodded.

"I was able to figure out that he was in Denver. I flew here Tuesday. Yesterday morning I kept the building under surveillance until a blond with a yellow purse showed up. I intercepted her and asked her if she was wearing a white skirt and white blouse on Monday. She said she was. I told her she was being stalked. You know the rest."

"Interesting."

She tightened her brow.

"You don't believe me."

Teffinger shifted his feet.

"Do you still have your plane ticket?"

She pulled it out of her purse.

It was legitimate, a one-way ticket for Kovi-Ke Gray from Jamaica to New York and a second from New York to Denver. She also had registration papers for the Sheraton, checking in Tuesday night.

He handed them back.

"Where were you Monday when you had the vision?"

"Jamaica. Underwater, diving. I own a dive shop in Montego Bay called the Ugly Tuna. I was escorting four divers when the vision came. We were in the Throne Room, actually."

"What's that?"

"The Throne Room? It's an underwater cavern about sixty-five feet down. The walls are covered with yellow sponges and coral. You get to it through a crack in the reef about eight feet wide. There's a large elephant ear sponge on the bottom that looks like a throne."

Teffinger pictured it and winced.

"Sounds claustrophobic."

"It's not for everyone. You need to be wired for it, which is why I usually take it, that and the Widowmaker's Cave, where you enter eighty feet down and then come up and out through a ten-foot-wide chimney. Or you can go the other direction, although that's not my preference. I have other divers who work for me that primarily only take groups to the City that Sank."

"Which is what?"

"You're not a diver, are you?"

"Not exactly."

"The City that Sank is the old Port Royal," she said. "It used to be a pirate hub way back in the day, frequented by the likes of Anne Bonny and Mary Read. Pirates congregated there from as far away as Madagascar. In 1692 an earthquake destroyed the city and caused about two-thirds of it to sink into the sea, including several pirate ships. It's a relatively open dive if you want it to be, so you don't have to be as experienced to do it. It's my bread and butter."

"So you have people who work for you?"

"We have three boats and several dive leaders," she said. "We're in negotiations with the government to harvest the pirate ships I told you about."

"So, archeological work?"

"If it pans out."

The sunshine hammered down.

"I need coffee," he said. "You want some?" She hesitated. "Don't worry about Station. She won't be out for at least a couple of hours."

5

June 5
Thursday Morning

They ended up down at the BNSF switchyard, sitting on the tailgate of his Tundra with a thermos of coffee and disposable cups in hand. The clanging of couplers and the power of the engines were their wind chimes. Teffinger pointed to a nearby building, an abandoned, boarded-up four-story brick job, and said, "A guy named Tarzan used to live there."

"Who was he?"

"A guy with ambition, but not the right kind. More the kind that gets you dead."

"He's dead?"

"No but he will be someday. I like to come here now and then to remind myself he's still walking the earth." He took a long sip and said, "So how do you know this guy's a killer? Have you seen him actually kill anyone?"

"No but I've seen his handiwork."

"Meaning what, exactly?"

She retreated in thought.

Her face grew tense.

"A woman was lying on the ground on her back," she said. "She wasn't moving. Her stomach was exposed and he was staring at it—meaning I was staring at it through his eyes. It wasn't moving, the way it would be if she were breathing. It was totally and absolutely still."

"So she looked dead."

"No, not looked, was," she said. "What happened next is that he wrote something on a piece of paper. I saw his hands in front of him as if they were my own. They were wearing latex gloves."

"What'd he write? Did you see?"

"Yes. He was using a pencil. He wrote, 16 Weeks. He did it in block lettering, not his normal handwriting, real slow, as if forcing himself to not use his usual writing. What happened next is the freaky part."

"Why, what happened?"

"He folded the paper until it was only about two inches long," she said. "Then he rolled it up until it was shaped like a cigarette, and he put it inside a glass vial about three inches long. He screwed a cap on. Then he cut a slit in the woman's stomach and shoved the vial in." She exhaled. "That's when my vision stopped."

"Did you see the victim's face?"

"No," she said. "When I'm looking through his eyes I can only see what he sees. It's not like I'm there next to him and can look around wherever I want. He didn't look at her face, at least not right then."

"Tell me about her stomach."

"It was tight, in good shape. I would say she was under thirty for sure."

"White?"

She nodded.

"White but tanned."

"When did this happen?"

"The vision? About a month ago," she said. "Here's the funny part though. You asked me before if I see things in real time. When I saw the guy stalking Station on Monday, that was pretty much real time. It came to me shortly before noon, which was about ten Denver time. That's when Station came to work. The sounds and the picture fit together. The stomach girl, though, I don't think that was in real time."

"Why not?"

"Because the visual of her was mixed together with a visual of the inside of a restaurant. It was like I was watching TV and flicking between channels. He couldn't have been in both places at the same time. I think he was in a restaurant at the time and thinking about what he did at an earlier time."

"So you were seeing his thoughts?"

She shrugged.

"Yes and no. I was getting the visual part of his thoughts. I never get feelings or emotions or complicated thoughts or what he's planning or anything like that. What I get is a lot more stripped down, like what you'd get from a video camera, meaning visual and audio and that's it. I think I was picking up the visual part of a memory he was replaying in his mind at a later time." She cast her eyes on the building where Tarzan lived. "Can we go in there?"

"Why?"

"I've never been in a killer's place."

Teffinger hopped off the tailgate.

"Sure, why not?"

She followed.

Then they headed for the building.

On the way he said, "How long have you been having these flashes?"

"Not long. They started about three months ago."

"So it's a recent thing—"

"Relatively."

"Did something happen in your life around that time?"

"Like what?"

He shrugged.

"I don't know, something traumatic; did you bump your head or did someone close to you die or something like that?"

She tensed.

Then she said, "No, nothing happened."

"So they just all of a sudden started?"

"Right."

6

June 5
Thursday Morning

Teffinger rolled a rusty 55-gallon drum under a window, pried plywood off with a piece of rebar, and gained entry to the building. Inside it was quiet with no signs of transient intrusion. Shafts of sunlight punched through dusty air. They took the stairs up to the top floor, which was an airy open space with distressed wooden plank floors, high ceilings and walls of windows, most of which were surprisingly intact.

"This is where Tarzan lived," he said. "Before he bought the place it was a shoe factory."

Kovi-Ke approached.

She came close, almost stomach-to-stomach.

"Keep your eyes open," she said. "Think about Tarzan for a minute. Don't think of anything else, only him."

"Why?"

"Please, do it for me."

Teffinger complied.

At first the images were vague. But as he remembered, they became more visual and burned deeper and deeper into his mind.

Kovi-Ke stepped back.

"You want to kill him," she said.

"Now you're reading my mind?"

"No, I'm just looking into your eyes. What I see there is that you want to kill him."

Teffinger shrugged.

"Maybe."

"You would, if you got the chance; if you could justify it somehow, you'd do it."

"Maybe."

"There are no maybes," she said. "If you could justify it, if he was escaping or something like that, you'd take him down, you'd do it in a heartbeat and never look back. The world would be a better place."

"That last part's true, that's for sure."

"So is the first part. It's okay, I understand."

"Understand what?"

"The feeling. I wanted to be sure you did too, before I tell you what I'm going to tell you."

"Which is what, exactly?"

"Which is, that's how I feel."

"About the killer?"

She nodded.

"I don't want to see through his eyes anymore."

"Killing someone is never the right answer."

She came close, with her lips almost touching his. "You're not in his head. If you were, you'd understand better. But that's only half of it. The other half is that I'm pretty sure he's in my head the same way I'm in his."

"You mean he can see through your eyes?"

She put her arms around his neck.

"Yes, sporadically."

"What makes you think that?"

"It's just a feeling I get," she said. "It's like there's a shadow in my head." She paused and added, "He's trying to figure out who I am."

"Why?"

"So he can kill me."

She spun off and broke into a dance, an unashamed, hypnotic dance, so entrancing that it filled Teffinger's eyes and brain and soul with a hunger he'd never felt before.

He wanted her.

There was nothing else in the world, only her.

It made no sense.

She was more wrong for him than almost any woman on earth.

It didn't matter.

She was like a rock to the head. Smack, there you go, now deal with it, not in ten seconds, now, right now in this nanosecond of your life.

She pulled the baseball hat off, released her ponytail and shook her hair loose. Nothing sexier had ever happened on the face of the earth.

She unbuttoned her shirt and threw it across the room.

Then she took off her bra, waved it over her head and tossed it to Teffinger. He caught it and draped it over his shoulder.

It was his now.

No one else had it, only him.

Then he went to her.

She was waiting for him.

She was waiting for him with every molecule of life in

her sinful little body.

7

June 5
Thursday Morning

Back at homicide, Teffinger was in trouble and knew it. Kovi-Ke was a sudden drug in his life and he was already addicted. She was a bad drug, one that would kill him; he didn't know that for sure, but that was his sense. Either way, he didn't care. He'd die with the taste of her on his tongue and the sins of her legs wrapped around his body.

He headed for the coffee, only to be intercepted by Sydney Heatherwood, the newbie of the department, hand stolen by Teffinger out of vice a year ago. Her mocha African-American skin played well against a crisp white blouse and the tautness of her athletic body couldn't be denied.

"You look weird," she said. "You're up to something."

He poured milk in a cup, topped it with coffee and took a noisy slurp.

"Do me a favor and pull the Tarzan file."

She frowned.

"He's long gone, give it up."

"Please and thank you."

"You're chasing shadows."

"Actually, the opposite."

At his desk he dialed Dr. Leigh Sandt, the FBI profiler in Quantico, who actually answered with a live human voice instead of a recorded one. He pulled up an image of a classy fiftyish woman with Tina Turner legs and a wedding ring the size of a small planet.

"It's me," he said.

"Teff?"

"Yes. I need a favor."

"No, no favors," she said. "You did something and didn't tell me about it."

"What'd I do?"

"Let me give you a hint," she said. "It's sitting on the corner of my desk. It has the initials GQ on it."

"Oh, that."

He'd almost forgotten about it. GQ was doing a spread called GQs On The Street. They snapped his photo one day down on the 16th Street Mall, did a short interview and had him sign a release, with no promises he'd be used. That was over two months ago. He'd never heard from them since.

"I can't believe you're on the cover of GQ and don't even tell me."

"I'm on the cover?"

"Are you telling me you didn't know?"

"Not really, but listen, it's not important. What is important is that I'm trying to find out if there's anyone out there who slits a woman's stomach open after he kills her and shoves in a glass vial. There would be a piece of paper in the vial."

"Like a note or something?"

"A piece of paper, folded and then rolled. It would say, 16 Weeks."

"16 Weeks?"

"Right."

"What's it mean?"

"I have no idea," he said. "To tell you the truth, I doubt that it even exists."

She called back two hours later and said, "Alley Savannah." The words were a two-by-four to the side of Teffinger's head. "She was stabbed in the back of the neck in Miami almost exactly two years ago. The guy you want to talk to is Lance Black. He's the detective in charge. Here's his number. Got a pencil?"

He did; he did indeed.

"Thanks, I owe you one."

"One? What kind of math are you using?"

He smiled.

"It's called Teffinger math."

"Well, you ought to bottle it and sell it. I know I'd buy some."

"I'll send you a free six pack."

Thirty seconds later he was on the phone with Detective Lance Black who confirmed everything with one minor clarification, "There was a bit of a space between the 1 and the 6. It might be 1 space 6 instead of 16."

"Maybe he had prior victims and number 1, his first one, he kept for 6 weeks."

"Could be. Whatever it means, we never figured it out."

"Who knows about the vial and the note?"

"If you mean, was it ever made public, the answer is no."

"It didn't get leaked?"

"No. That's not the question though. The question is how do you know about it?"

Teffinger tightened.

"It's complicated."

"It's complicated?"

"Yes."

"As in, you're not going to tell me what's going on?"

Teffinger exhaled.

"Look, I don't want to be an asshole, but my gut's telling me this is going to play out better if it's not done in pieces. Let me work it. I'll give you everything you're looking for when the timing is right."

"Is that final?"

"I'm sorry. I'm an ass."

"No one's ever kept me out before," Black said. "If it was anyone but you, I'd be upset."

"What's that mean?"

"It means I was one of the three hundred people at your seminar in New York last year." He paused and added, "Let me ask you one thing, though."

"Sure."

"Did you get the information from a female?"

Teffinger cleared his throat.

"Yes."

"Then you're talking to the killer," Black said. "The victim was strictly into girls. She was at a lesbian bar the night she disappeared, a place called Blackbird Ordinary. I've expected a female killer from day one."

Teffinger pictured it.

It wasn't pretty.

"Can you send me the file?"

"It's on the way. Give me your email address." Teffinger did and Black added, "Be careful. I don't know what kind of game she's playing but you're obviously smack dab in it."

"I'll be in touch." He almost powered off and added, "Are you still there?"

"Yes."

"The seminar, was it any good?"

"Let me put it this way," Black said. "I was sitting next to Lori Bender, a newbie who isn't all that hard on the eyes, if you catch my drift. She just about had an orgasm watching you. That's as close to sex with her as I'll ever get, so in a way I owe you one. The donuts weren't bad, either."

"So, two out of three?"

"Right. And that ain't bad, at least according to Meat Loaf."

8

June 5
Thursday Afternoon

According to the file, Alley Savannah disappeared exactly two years to the day, on June 5; far too precise to be a coincidence. So what was Kovi-Ke's game? Was she in town to kill someone else right under a detective's nose? Was she trying to get Teffinger so lust-drunk that he couldn't think straight?

One thing was for sure.

Station was the target.

On second thought, wait. Maybe Station was a decoy. Maybe someone else was the target. Maybe it was even Teffinger himself. In a crazy way that actually makes sense. She gets him all caught up in what's going on with Station and then—wham!—she takes him when his head's down between her legs.

If that was the case though, how did she pick him out?

Did she see his photo on GQ?

Was that it?

Did she tap her finger on his face and say, You're next, baby. Say bye-bye.

A file suddenly plopped on his desk, the Tarzan file, compliments of Sydney who said, "You look like you just ate a ghost."

He didn't doubt it.

"Do you have time to do a little project?"

She looked skeptical.

"As in what?"

"Kovi-Ke Gray," he said. "I need everything you can get on her." He told her what he knew; she was from Jamaica, ran a dive shop called the Ugly Tuna, was negotiating with the Jamaican government to harvest pirate ships, etcetera. "Go deep. Oh, and pay particular attention to whether she has any ties to Miami or a lesbian bar called Blackbird Ordinary. If she was in Miami in June two years ago, I'd really like to know it. She may have killed someone down there and she might be in Denver to do a repeat."

He headed downtown on foot, a ten-minute jaunt through buzz and congestion. His heart raced and confusion ricocheted inside his skull. Even with everything he knew about Kovi-Ke, he couldn't push her out. She was in him, in his blood, in his breath, and in the deep, dark, secret parts of his brain, not to mention the nasty parts.

The sun bounced off his face.

It was a constant, an old friend.

Kovi-Ke.

Kovi-Ke.

Kovi-Ke.

He turned the final corner, hoping to find her where he first saw her this morning, staking out Station.

She was there.

The corner of his mouth turned up ever so slightly as he headed over.

"How's the hunt going?"

"Not good."

"Nothing?"

"Not yet."

Teffinger shifted his feet and said, "Alley Savannah. Does that name ring a bell?"

"No. Should it?"

"I did a little research," he said. "She's the stomach girl, the one you told me about."

"So she's real?"

"Was," he said. "You said your vision was a month ago."

"That's right."

"She was killed two years ago, exactly two years ago as a matter of fact, on June fifth. Maybe your friend is on a schedule."

Kovi-Ke didn't hesitate.

"He's going to take Station tonight. We have to do something."

Teffinger nodded.

"We will," he said. "What other visions have you had of the guy murdering someone? Any?"

She nodded.

"I think so."

"Tell me about them."

A strange expression washed over her face, almost as if she was sinking into a trance.

"Are you okay?"

She said nothing.

He shook her shoulders, "Kovi-Ke."

She looked at him but it was vague.

Then she focused and locked her eyes on him for several seconds. Her expression pulled back to normal and she said, "This isn't good."

"What isn't?"

"I think he was just in my head. He was looking right at you."

9

June 5
Thursday Afternoon

Deep down Teffinger had to admit that the words—He was looking right at you—were unsettling, but not because there was someone behind Kovi-Ke's eyes looking at him. That wasn't possible. What was possible, however, is that Kovi-Ke was turning her plan tighter on Teffinger, getting closer to killing him. The so-called vision was nothing more than a ruse to try to shift the blame to someone else now that the act was approaching.

In a way that was good.

Station wasn't the target.

Teffinger was.

Station was safe.

On second thought, that might not be totally true. Kovi-Ke might kill Station as a way to pretend that there really was a killer in town.

Damn it.

Every time Teffinger thought he had it figured out, it twisted away. He'd wrestled greased strippers that weren't half as slippery.

His phone rang and a man's voice came through, "Long time, huh?" Teffinger vaguely recognized the intonation but couldn't place it. "You don't know who this is?"

"No."

"Wow, I'm crushed. I thought I owned a bigger part of your brain than that."

"So who am I talking to?"

"Time, that's the thing to be most afraid of. Time makes everything fade. It turns everything to shadows. The secret is to always be replacing the old things with new ones. Keep the colors bright. Keep the sounds crisp. That's what I'm doing, replacing the old things with new ones."

"Tarzan?"

"There you go," the man said. "Now it's starting to come back. Congratulations on the GQ cover. You're looking good. It reminded me that we hadn't talked for a long time. Let's get a beer sometime. My treat."

The connection died.

The number was blocked. Teffinger dialed Sydney, explained what just happened and talked to her about seeing if Forensics could figure out where the call came from; the number, the geographical location, whatever their magic could get.

"They might need your phone."

"Let me know."

He hung up.

"What's going on?"

The words came from Kovi-Ke.

"That was Tarzan."

"They same one as this morning?"

"Yes."

"That's weird. Is he in Denver?"

"I don't know."

"He must be," she said.

"Why?"

"It's too much of a coincidence that you go into his place in the morning and then get a call from him in the afternoon. He must have seen you."

Teffinger chewed on it.

It had no taste.

"There's no reason for him to be anywhere near his old place," he said. "We've already scoured it. So has the FBI."

"You missed something," she said.

"That's not possible."

"You missed something important enough for him to come back for it."

"Like what?"

"I don't know."

Suddenly she gasped.

Her face tensed.

Her body froze.

"I'm in his head!" she said. "I'm seeing out his eyes."

"Right now?"

"He's walking. He's following a blond woman. She's about thirty steps in front of him," she said. "I think it's Station, but how could it be? She never left the building. I've been right here all afternoon."

"What's she wearing?"

"A black T-shirt and white shorts," she said.

"That's not what she was wearing this morning."

"Wait! Yes, it's her. It's definitely her. She just stopped.

She's looking in a window. She's taking off her sunglasses to see something better. The man has stopped. He's looking around. The buildings are high. They must be right around here somewhere."

"Are there shuttle-buses?"

"Yes."

"That's the 16th Street Mall."

"She's walking again," she said. "So is he. She's crossing a street. The sign says California."

"That's definitely the mall."

"Whoa!"

"What happened?"

"She almost got hit! A red car just slammed to a stop and almost took her out! I'm looking at the driver. It's a white girl, a teenager with punk hair—pink. Three guys are in the car with her. They're all wearing black. It's fading. It's gone now. I'm out." She swallowed. "I think he knew I was there."

Teffinger pulled Station's business card out of his wallet and dialed her cell. She answered on the second ring. "It's me, Teffinger. Where are you?"

"Walking home."

"On the mall?"

"Yes."

"What are you wearing?"

"Why?"

"Just indulge me."

"Shorts."

"What color?"

"White."

"Are you wearing a black T-shirt too?"

"Yes."

"Did a car almost hit you?"

Silence.

"Are you following me or something?"

"No, just answer the question."

"Yes."

"Where?"

"At California."

"Tell me about it."

"I'm okay, it didn't hit me."

"That's not what I'm getting at," he said. "Describe the car."

"It was red, an older Camry I think."

"Who was inside?"

"Teenagers," she said. "A girl and three boys."

"Was the girl driving?"

"Yes. She skidded to a stop. I'm okay."

"Tell me about her?"

"She was punked up, with pink hair. I don't understand what's going on."

"Look behind you," he said. "See if someone's following you about thirty steps behind."

"There are a lot of people."

"It would be a man by himself," Teffinger said.

"A guy just turned off. He stared at me for a second when I looked at him and then he veered off."

"Don't follow him! What's he wearing?"

"A red baseball hat, sunglasses, jeans."

"What about the shirt?"

"It's green. He looks strong. A shuttle just stopped right next to me."

"Get on it and get out of there!"

Teffinger hung up, grabbed Kovi-Ke's hand and headed for the mall at a trot.

"What kind of car almost hit Station?"

"It was older," she said. "A Camry I think." Then she pointed. "There it is! That's it right there!"

It was right next to them, stopped at a light.

Inside was a punked-out blond and three guys in black.

Teffinger stopped long enough to memorize the license plate and then kept going.

10

June 5
Thursday Afternoon

The afternoon was a flurry of motion but whether that motion was forwards or backwards only time would tell. Station hired two security men—guys personally known to Teffinger—and promised to keep them with her day and night until Teffinger said otherwise.

The man following Station was long gone by the time Teffinger got there. Several security cameras in the area shined on the guy but none showed his face thanks to the baseball cap. They did show that his arms were pythons and his chest was steel. In a fair fight Teffinger would be able to hold his own but not for long.

Was he Tarzan?

It was possible.

It was very possible.

Tarzan's mane could have been tucked up under the hat, or cut off by this point, although Teffinger doubted the latter. The mane was too much a part of Tarzan's being. He'd cut off an ear before the mane.

Had Kovi-Ke actually seen through the eyes of the guy?

The details were extensive and verified by security cameras, including Station stopping to look in a window and taking off her sunglasses, almost getting hit by the Camry at California, and wearing the clothes as described. She'd snuck out the back of the building; that's why Kovi-Ke didn't see her leave. She'd changed into different clothes before she left.

Teffinger didn't want to believe it was possible.

His initial inclination was to look for something that could be explained. Possibly Station and Kovi-Ke were in some kind of conspiracy with each other. While good in theory, the facts didn't pan out. When Teffinger questioned Station about whether she knew Kovi-Ke, the concept was so strange that the woman didn't even know how to respond.

No, no, no.

She didn't know Kovi-Ke.

She had no idea what was going on.

The truth of what she was saying resonated in Teffinger's gut.

She wasn't lying.

Also, there was the little fact that Station almost got run over crossing California. Even if Station and Kovi-Ke were in some type of cahoots for some unexplained reason, that external incident was seen by Kovi-Ke in real time and was unexplainable unless the punk girl driver was also in the mix. From the license plate, Teffinger tracked her down and interviewed her. She didn't know Station or Kovi-Ke and wasn't part of the mix. She was just an art student who got a little reckless while driving and that was the beginning and end of it.

No, there was no conspiracy going on.

Early evening alone in the office, Teffinger was surprised when the door opened and Sydney walked in. "Got something you'll be interested in," she said.

"Like what."

She dropped three pieces of paper on his desk and then took a seat as he read them.

They appeared to be a police report filed by Kovi-Ke in Port-au-Prince, Haiti, in February of this year, four months ago. According to the report, she was drugged and abducted from something called Karnaval and taken to some remote beach location for some type of hard-core voodoo ritual that lasted all night. She was finally dumped in the trunk of a car and released naked and traumatized just outside the city an hour before the sun came up. She never got a good look at anyone involved, with the exception of one man who approached her just as she was starting to lose consciousness; the guy who abducted her; a nice-looking guy with dreadlocks.

Teffinger looked up.

"Is this real?"

"Yes."

Teffinger dropped the papers.

"Kovi-Ke said her visions started three months ago. That would have been a month after this happened."

"You think she was cursed or something?"

Teffinger shook his head.

"I don't know what to think."

Sydney's phone rang. She listened, hung up and said, "Okay, that call you got from Tarzan this afternoon, it was from one of those pre-paid jobs, purchased with cash in Miami two months ago. Here's the interesting part. The call was placed from Denver."

Teffinger nodded.

"So, he's in town."

"It looks that way."

Miami.

Miami.

Miami.

Why did the word bounce in Teffinger's brain?

Then it came to him.

That's where the stomach girl was murdered two years ago.

Miami.

"Tarzan's the guy stalking Station," he said. "Let's get a BOLO out on him, statewide."

"You want to do it or do you want me to?"

Teffinger stood up.

"You do it. I'm going to make a run."

"To where?"

"It's better you don't know."

11

June 5
Thursday Night

Teffinger got home just before dark to find a surprise, namely Kovi-Ke sitting on his front steps. He handed her the Haiti police report, unlocked the front door and stepped in.

She followed.

"Did you make that report?"

"Yes."

"What it says there, did it really happen?"

"Yes."

He exhaled.

"Tell me about it."

With that, she told him a story so detailed it was as if he was right there.

* * * * *

After passing out at Karnaval, she regained consciousness at some point later, which could have been two minutes or two days, to find herself on her back on sand in the middle of the night, staked out inside a ring of torches. Drums beat but they weren't Karnaval drums. They were evil. They pounded with a devil's hand.

She pulled wildly at her bonds.

The ropes dug into her wrists and ankles, ready to tear her flesh if she pulled even a breath harder. She put every muscle of her body into it.

The ropes didn't budge.

They drew blood.

They had her.

They had her good.

Her chest pounded.

The torches were blinding suns in her eyes making it almost impossible to see beyond. Still, she was able to catch fleeting glimpses of painted faces, demon masks and crazed dancing. The men were bare-chested. The women were too, shaking their breasts and hips with a possessed abandon.

She was in some kind of voodoo ritual.

She'd heard about them.

There were rumors all throughout the Caribbean.

They had always had been there, even when she was little.

She'd never believed them or, if she had, thought they were nothing more than exaggerations of scary things out of the past, put into young minds where they fermented and hardened and turned into dark places where they dared not go even as adults.

Suddenly a hand appeared from behind her and held her head immobile. Another hand pulled her jaw down and her mouth open. A snake appeared above her, dangled from above with its fangs mere inches from her eyes.

It lingered there, second after second after second, twisting for its life.

Then a machete swung from out of the shadows and lopped the head off.

It bounced off her nose and fell to the side.

The body above stopped wiggling. Blood and guts dripped out, at first into her eyes, then onto her lips and into her mouth.

She pulled at the ropes with all her strength.

It did no good.

12

June 5

Thursday Night

Teffinger's blood raced. "I asked you point blank before if anything happened in your life like an accident or someone dying or something like that," he said. "You said no." Kovi-Ke's eyes darted. "You lied to me. You lied right to my face."

"So what was I supposed to say? That I got some kind of a voodoo curse put on me?"

"Well, it's true, isn't it?"

She shrugged.

"If I said that, you'd think I was even crazier than you already thought I was. You wouldn't have given me the time of day. Station would be dead by now."

Teffinger pulled two beers from the fridge, handed one to Kovi-Ke and took a long ice-cold swallow from his. His brain softened. The pressure in his veins reigned back.

Kovi-Ke wrapped her arms around him and laid her head on his chest.

"The Caribbean isn't the United States," she said. "It's old and superstitious, there are secrets there, and there's a darkness that covers that whole part of the world like a blanket. It has things, evil things, that can't be explained and shouldn't be real but probably are."

"Like voodoo?"

"The stories are always there and always have been there," she said. "You hear them since you were a kid. I never believed them, at least not in the logical part of my brain. There's a deep part of your soul though where they get in and never come out. It would be hard to understand if you didn't grow up with it."

Teffinger took a long swallow.

"We have the same thing here," he said. "It's called the boogieman."

Kovi-Ke shook her head.

"Don't patronize me. This is different. A lot of people in that part of the world—all kinds of people, including respected ones—believe in voodoo and occult and shadows. They talk about it. They embrace it or accept it or avoid it, but either way it's something real. Like I said, I never really fully believed in it. I'm still not sure I do."

"Even after the curse?"

"I'm not sure I was cursed."

"Then how do you see through someone's eyes? What other explanation is there?"

"I'm not saying that what's happening to me now doesn't go back to that night," she said. "It has to. You're right, there is no other explanation. What I'm saying is, I'm not sure the curse was on me. The more I think about it, the more I think it was on him."

"Meaning what?"

"Meaning I've been put in motion to bring him down. I'm the devil of death as far as he's concerned."

Teffinger drained what as left of the beer and pulled another. "Put in motion by who?"

"Unknown."

"You must have some idea," Teffinger said.

She took a sip of beer, made a face and set it on the table. Then she lit a joint and inhaled long and deep.

"When I made the police report, I knew before I even left the building that nothing would ever come of it. They went through motions afterwards, as if they were investigating, but they weren't."

"And why not?"

"My guess? Because they were scared."

"Of what?"

"Repercussions; I'm not sure what kind—curses, murder, devils, burning in hell, who knows what. Make up whatever you want, something real though. Something deep down that they can't deny."

"Did you ever tell them you could see through someone's eyes?"

She shook her head.

"That didn't start for a month afterwards so I had nothing to say when I made the report. Afterwards, like I said, they didn't want anything to do with it."

Teffinger opened an image on his cell phone, an image of a man six-four with a chiseled body, rugged jungle looks and a long mane of thick blond hair.

"Have you ever seen this guy?"

"No."

"Look carefully, his hair might be cut off now or dyed."

"I've never seen him," she said. "I can guarantee you that.

I'm good with faces. Is that Tarzan?"

"Yes."

"I don't think I'm seeing through his eyes."

"Why not?"

"I don't know. It just doesn't feel right." She paused and added, "What'd he do, anyway?"

Teffinger hardened his face.

"I'm not at liberty to get into it."

"Come on, Teffinger. I showed you mine. Show me yours."

"I'll tell you after he makes me kill him."

"And when will that be?"

"Hopefully, tonight."

Outside the wind kicked up.

Dark clouds were blowing in.

A storm was in the making.

"This is good," he said.

"Why?"

"It fits the night that's about to be." He swallowed what was left of his beer. "I'm going to take a shower. Then I'm going to go to Tarzan's and wait for him. You're going to stay here."

"No I'm not," she said. "I'm coming with you."

Teffinger shook his head.

"Out of the question."

"Maybe I'm wrong," she said. "Maybe it is his eyes that I see out of. If that's true, I might get a flash. It might save your life."

"I don't care about my life all that much."

"Well, then you're alone in that regard. I'm coming with you. You can either take me or I'll go there on my own. I know where it's at, remember? Either way, I'm going."

Two minutes later Teffinger stepped into the shower, got the water as hot as he could stand it and let the questions bounce in his brain. One grew larger than the others.

Was Kovi-Ke going to kill him tonight?

13

13

June 5
Thursday Night

After dark Teffinger parked the Tundra a quarter mile away from Tarzan's lair and stepped out into a black, nasty storm. Lightning arced across an evil sky, strobe-lighting eerie industrial silhouettes. He hunched against the weather, already soaked. The beers that tasted so good earlier in the evening now sat dull and dead in his gut. His body ached. His eyes wanted to close and stay that way for the rest of his life.

He fought through it all.

At the building he entered through the same place as this afternoon, then climbed the stairs in the dark without a flashlight to the top floor, made his way to the far corner and slumped down.

He was alone.

Kovi-Ke wasn't with him.

He wasn't about to bring a civilian into a potentially dangerous situation.

The corner felt good.

It was safe.

The radiant warmth of the day still resonated there.

Tarzan was a ladies' man. He could charm a woman even as strong and exotic as Kovi-Ke. Plus they'd both arrived in Denver at the same time, give or take. Because of that alone, Teffinger couldn't discount that maybe the two of them were in some kind of a conspiracy. But if so, to do what?

To kill him?

He shook his head.

Why was he always jumping to the worst-case scenario? Why was he hell-bent on believing Kovi-Ke was out to get him? Sure, he had facts that pointed that way, but in his gut he couldn't deny that something deeper was at work.

He could love her.

He could do it completely and absolutely.

That scared him.

He'd be vulnerable.

A sound came, barely audible over the storm but something out of step with the rest of the night, something that didn't belong, maybe something innocent from the rail yard but just as easily maybe something more sinister. He held his breath and focused.

It didn't reappear, not in five seconds or ten or a full minute.

He couldn't make it come back.

Devil of death.

Kovi-Ke's words hadn't left Teffinger's brain, not once since she uttered them; not because they were so strangely poetic but because they represented a theory that might actually be in play. It was possible that the curse—to the extent there really was one—was on the man instead of Kovi-Ke.

Either way, whoever put the curse into motion knew who the man was. Whoever orchestrated the night of voodoo knew who the man was.

Wait a minute, maybe he didn't.

Maybe he or she or they knew of the man but didn't know his exact identity. Maybe that's why they brought Kovi-Ke into the mix, to find out who he was.

Still, they had some kind of connection to him.

They had pieces of the puzzle.

Teffinger checked his watch, added two hours and concluded that the FBI profiler, Dr. Leigh Sandt, had long since gone to bed.

He called her anyway.

"I know I'm waking you up and I'm going to hell for it," he said.

"Teffinger?"

"I need to know something. Do we have any people in Haiti that I can tap?"

"If you mean FBI, no."

"How about CIA?"

"I'm sure there's CIA there but that's not my circle."

"Can you get me a name and number?"

"God, Teffinger—"

Suddenly a noise came from down below, somewhere inside the building. Teffinger killed the power on the phone, stood up and drew his gun.

Then he stood perfectly still.

14

June 5
Thursday Night

The beam of a flashlight bounced off the walls, making its way up the final stairs and into the room. Teffinger's heart raced.

"Teffinger!"

The voice wasn't rough.

It was Jamaican.

"Over here," he said.

The light shined on him, then dropped out of his eyes and onto the floor as it made its way over. Then it went out. Kovi-Ke wrapped her arms around his neck and whispered in his ear, "Looks like I was telling the truth about coming."

"You shouldn't have," Teffinger said. "Now I have to abort."

"Go ahead but I'm staying here."

Teffinger exhaled.

"This isn't a game."

She held her arms out and said, "Search me."

"Why?"

"Because I don't have a gun, I don't have a knife, I don't

even have a paperclip," she said.

"Why would I care?"

"We both know why. Do it."

He did it, running his hands over her body, at first all business, then more personal, more private, more in a way that made her spread her legs ever so slightly.

"I'm not in town to kill you," she said. "Get used to the idea."

"I never said you were."

"You thought it." A beat then, "I made love to you this morning, in case you didn't notice."

"I noticed."

"So what'd you think, that that was some kind of a black widow thing?"

"No."

"Don't be afraid of me," she said. "It hurts me when you are."

Teffinger wrapped his arms around her and pulled her tight. Her chest beat against his, the wetness of her clothes felt like a thousand ancient genes running through his blood.

He kissed her.

It was wrong.

The timing was bad.

He didn't care.

She kissed him back, deeper, longer, suddenly an animal, not to be denied for even a second longer. She ripped his shirt open, then her own, and pressed her breasts against him.

The storm pounded down with an aching fury.

Lightning flashed.

Every molecule in Teffinger's brain exploded.

He dropped to his knees and yanked down her shorts.

Then a sound came, not from them, from below, somewhere down in the guts of the building, a sound that could have been a crowbar or piece of rebar dropping to the floor.

He froze.

"Did you hear that?"

"Hear what?"

He pulled his gun and said, "Stay here. Don't move from this spot. I need to know exactly where you are. Tell me!"

"I'll stay here."

He kissed her, made his way to the stairs and headed down on slow cat feet.

His heart pounded.

Tarzan could kill him in a fair fight.

It couldn't get to that point.

Not for a second.

The third floor was blacker than black when he got to it. Unlike the top floor, the windows were minimal. The thickness of the storm beat away the few lights that otherwise could have shined in from the rail yard. He might as well have been a hundred miles under the ground in a locked vault.

No sounds came.

No flashlights flickered.

He headed lower, to the second floor.

It was a repeat, dark and lifeless.

He descended to the ground floor.

It was another repeat.

Then suddenly a window shattered, from an outside rock or chunk of asphalt that bounced across the floor and skidded to a stop. Teffinger carefully made his way over and peered out.

Thirty yards away, by the black silhouette of a railcar, a flashlight turned on and pointed directly at him. It flicked back and forth, almost as if daring him to come out and see who was behind it.

The space between the building and flashlight was open.

There were no poles or dumpsters.

He'd be exposed.

What to do?

Go out the back and circle around?

Then something happened he didn't expect. A voice shouted over the storm, "See you soon, Teffinger!"

He knew that voice.

He knew it only too well.

"Tarzan!"

"Tell me something. That island girl you're screwing, is she as good as she looks?"

"Tarzan!"

No reply came.

"Tarzan!"

15

June 5
Thursday Night

Tarzan was gone, not to return, not tonight at least. Teffinger made his way through the storm to the Tundra with his left arm wrapped around Kovi-Ke's waist and the cold steel of his weapon gripped in his right hand.

Twenty minutes later they were home.

There he swallowed a beer, called in the incident to dispatch and made sure a renewed BOLO was put out on Tarzan. Tomorrow he'd go back to the lair to try to figure out if Tarzan had beaten him there and already extracted whatever it was he came back for.

But why was he screwing with Teffinger?

Why did he call him?

Why did he taunt him with the flashlight?

Was it all a sick little foreplay to Teffinger's murder?

He was on the couch in the dark with the lights out and the storm beating every structure and road and car and streetlight and stray dog with evil fists, waiting for Tarzan to make another move, although it would be a long shot tonight.

Kovi-Ke was next to him, her soaking clothes replaced with a long-sleeve shirt out of Teffinger's closet. Underneath it was nothing except her. A glass of white perched in her lap.

Teffinger hardened his heart to be able to get through the next few minutes, which needed to be gotten through. "Island girl," he said. "That's what Tarzan called you."

"Yes."

"He knows you. He wouldn't say island unless he knew you were from one. That's not the kind of word that just pops into a sentence by accident."

"So, he knows me."

"Do you know him?"

"No."

"Are you sure?"

"Yes. It's not his eyes I see out of."

"How do you know?"

"I don't know, I just do. He's probably been stalking you. That's how he's seen me. Maybe he got close enough to hear my voice."

Teffinger chewed on it.

He shook his head.

"No, no way."

"Maybe you weren't there," she said. "Maybe I was talking to someone else."

She suddenly got very still.

"What's wrong?" Teffinger said.

"He was there!"

"Where?"

"Up on the top floor, somewhere in the dark. We weren't alone. He was there with us. He was right there! I had a creepy feeling. I thought it was just the storm and the whole weirdness of the place. But that's what it was. He was there."

Teffinger couldn't deny the possibility.

He hadn't brought a flashlight.

He'd never searched the place.

"If that was the case, why wouldn't he just take me out?"

"I don't know. Probably for the same reason he didn't take you out when he lured you down to the first floor. Whatever he's up to, it's not time yet."

Teffinger went to the window, drew the curtain ever so slightly and peeked out. Nothing was out there, only the storm.

Tarzan knew Kovi-Ke.

Did she know him, in spite of denying it?

Teffinger wasn't sure.

He still couldn't read her good enough.

He curled up on the couch with his head on the woman's lap.

His eyes closed.

If she killed him while he was sleeping, he didn't care.

He was too tired to care.

DAY THREE

June 6
Friday

16

June 6
Friday Morning

Teffinger woke just before the first rays of dawn Friday morning. No one had killed him during the night; not Tarzan, not Kovi-Ke, not Tarzan and Kovi-Ke in combination, not the crazy neighbor from down the street, not a 747 dropping out of the sky, no one. Right now, the way he felt, that was a good thing. Last night he didn't really care. Now he did.

He was on the couch with a pillow under his head.

He rocked to an upright position and headed to the bedroom to find Kovi-Ke sleeping on top of the sheets, still wearing his shirt, although now it had ridden up to her waist. He covered her with a blanket, gave her a soft kiss on the cheek and headed outside into the dark for a jog, making sure the door was solidly locked behind him.

Puddles were rampant and the air smelled like wet grass but the storm was gone.

Houses were dark.

Teffinger's body wasn't in the best of moods for a jog but that was too bad. It would need to comply. He put one foot in front of the other with a rhythm and let the streetlights click off. A dog behind a fence snapped off a half dozen warning barks as he passed. Something crossed the street up ahead, a cat or a fox, pausing briefly to size Teffinger up before it darted into the shadows and became forever gone.

Whatever it was it had survived the night.

Good job.

He picked up the pace; getting his knees higher and his stride longer and letting his lungs hunt deeper for air. The road went from downhill to flat to now slightly up, hardly up at all actually, but a strong anchor nonetheless. Teffinger forced his body to keep the speed up.

Kovi-Ke.

Kovi-Ke.

Kovi-Ke.

Who was she, really?

He got home half an hour later, three well-earned miles under the belt, to find the coffee pot warming up and the exotic little flower that was Kovi-Ke in the shower.

He stepped in, took the soap and worked it on her back, saying nothing.

Her hair was heavy with water.

Rogue strands danced back and forth on her neck from the spray.

Teffinger had never seen anything so pure and natural.

He kissed her there.

Everything in his world shifted; how big and how far, he wasn't sure yet—but a shift had come.

He whispered in her ear, "Tell me about the other murders."

"What do I get in return?"

"Whatever you want."

"What if what I want is you?"

"Then that's what you get," he said.

"Deal," she said. "Payment first."

"Now?"

She rubbed against him.

"Absolutely now."

He paid, and then over pancakes and coffee, she kept up her end. "Like I said before, I've never seen him actually kill anyone. All I've seen is the aftermath. The most disturbing one was the one I already told you about, the stomach girl."

"Alley Savannah."

"If that's her name."

"She was last seen at a lesbian club."

"Yeah, you told me." Teffinger must have had a look on his face because the woman added, "I've had women, if that's what your thinking."

Teffinger took a long slurp.

"That's not what I was thinking."

"Yes it was. That's okay. I'd be doing the same."

He took a noisy slurp of coffee.

"So you're bi?"

"I'm whatever I want to be at the moment. Life's too short to not take it, wherever it is." She smiled. "Do you have any lesbian girlfriends? You could bring her over and watch."

He pictured it.

"You're picturing it," she said.

He nodded.

"It's nice. Have you ever been to Miami?"

"Yes."

"Have you ever been to the club Alley Savannah was at?

The Blackbird Ordinary?"

She hesitated and then said, "Yes."

The word was a train slamming into Teffinger's chest.

"You have?"

"Yes."

"Why didn't you tell me about that before?"

"Because then you'd be focusing on me," she said. "I don't want you focusing on me. I want you focusing on the guy whose eyes I'm seeing out of. That's who killed her, not me."

"But you were there, at the club?"

"Once or twice but not that night or even that month. Like I said, I didn't kill her."

"Did you know her?"

"No."

"Did you see her there at the club when you were there?"

"If I did, I don't remember her."

"What do you remember?"

"I remember leaving with a curvy little blond," she said.

"Do you remember her name?"

"Yes."

"What was it?"

She hardened her face.

"I knew I shouldn't have told you anything. I gave you my body—twice—and you still don't trust me?"

"I trust you just fine," he said.

She dropped her fork and stood up.

"I'll tell you what," she said. "You contact me when that's actually true."

Then she was gone, out the door and gone, walking down the street and gone, leaving with a brisk stride and gone, all as Teffinger watched. His instinct was to chase her down.

He didn't.

He let her go.

It felt as if his arm had just fallen off.

At the office, Teffinger pulled Sydney into a private room and told her everything that was going on. She wasn't happy and wrinkled her face to prove it.

"Teff, your weakness is women and it always will be. We both know that. But this time you've gone too far."

"How do you figure?"

"Sleeping with her? It's against every rule in the book." Teffinger disagreed.

"She's not part of anything," he said.

"She's a witness," she said.

"How? By seeing out of someone's eyes? Try getting that in evidence in a court of law."

"She's a suspect," Sydney said.

"How?"

"Stop it Teffinger," she said. "Stop making excuses. However this case turns out, you've probably already blown it by sleeping with her."

"There is no case," he said.

"Then what do you call Station?"

"Station's fine," he said. "There's no crime involving her. The only possible case at play here involves Tarzan. He's already wanted. I could sleep with a million women and that wouldn't get him off the hook."

Sydney stood up.

"Rein yourself in," she said. "And don't come looking to me again for approval. You're not going to get it. What you're doing isn't okay and I'm not going to say it is."

She left.

Ten seconds later she was back.

"And while we're at it," she said, "laying in wait for Tarzan last night without telling anyone and without backup wasn't very smart."

"He would have seen backup," Teffinger said. "Going alone was our only shot."

She shook her head in disagreement.

"You had a civilian there too," she said. "You better stop and think about your actions because you're way over the line."

Then she was gone.

Ten seconds later she didn't come back.

He slumped back in the chair, alone, listening to the hum of the ceiling vent. When his phone rang he almost didn't answer, not needing yet a third thing to bite him. A woman's voice came through, one with a thick Caribbean accent.

"My name's Poppy and I'm with the CIA down here in Haiti," she said. "Leigh Sandt wanted me to give you a call. She said you need some information on a voodoo ritual that took place back in February during Karnaval."

"That's right. I appreciate your calling. Thank you."

"I'm not promising anything other than I'll sniff around to the extent I can," she said. "Tell me exactly what it is that you're looking for."

He did.

He wanted to know if it was true that a Jamaican woman by the name of Kovi-Ke was abducted and subjected to a voodoo ritual. If so, what happened during that ritual and more importantly who was behind it?

"This is going to sound stupid but is it possible to get cursed so that you see through someone else's eyes?"

"Yes."

The answer was without hesitation and wasn't what he expected.

"You really believe that?"

"It's not a matter of what I believe," she said. "It's a matter of what actually happens. That would be an extreme case but it wouldn't be impossible."

"I don't understand how."

"I appreciate the skepticism," she said. "I was where you are ten years ago. I'll be honest with you; voodoo is not something I like to get around. It's dangerous. It always knows that you're there before you know it is. I'll try to find out what you want but it might take some time."

"I understand."

"One more thing," she said. "Appreciate that Leigh pulled out a stop for you. This isn't the kind of thing we normally do."

"I won't forget her, or you," he said.

"I'll be in touch. Don't try to contact me, even through Leigh. When I get something I'll contact you. If I can't get anything I'll let you know that too. Either way I'll be in touch at some point."

"Thanks."

"You're welcome."

"Wait, are you still there?"

"Yes."

"I almost forgot to tell you, there's a guy called Tarzan who might be involved in all this. I have a full file on him."

"Send it to me through Leigh."

17

June 6
Friday Morning

Keep your friends close and your enemies closer, that's what everyone said. Teffinger didn't know which side of that equation Kovi-Ke fell on, but either way there was only one option. He dialed her and said, "Where are you?"

"A café across from Station's work."

"You're staking her out?"

"Yes."

"Stay there. I'm coming over."

He made the trip on foot in ten minutes, finding the woman at a table near the window with a cup of coffee waiting for him. He slid in, took a sip and said, "I'll be honest, I don't know if you killed Alley Savannah or not. I'm not going to lie to you. I owe you that much."

She shrugged.

"That's your dilemma, not mine."

"I had a crazy thought after you left this morning," he said. "Maybe you did it and you're blocking it out."

She shook her head.

"You just won't let it go, will you?"

"It happens," he said. "It's a psychological defense mechanism. Has anything like that ever happened to you, you know, where you found out after the fact that you did something but had no recollection of it?"

"No."

"Are you sure?"

She exhaled.

"I should never have told you that I'd been to the Blackbird. I thought we had a bond and that you trusted me. I thought I could open up."

"You can," he said.

She rolled her eyes.

"I'm taking this guy down with or without you," she said. "I don't care if you don't help, but don't get in the way."

Teffinger took a sip.

"Alright, let's do this," he said. "About ten times now you were going to tell me about some of the other killings. Tell me now. I'll see if I can run them down and figure out who they are, just like with Alley Savannah. If it turns out you have a good alibi for any one of them, then I'll know you're telling the truth. You still don't have an alibi for Alley, right?"

"From two years ago? Nothing that I remember as I sit here—"

"It was summer," Teffinger said. "Maybe you were doing a dive. Would there be papers, you know, a dive log or credit card receipts or something like that?"

"We're pretty loose on that kind of stuff but I could check when I get back to Jamaica," she said. "Right now I'm more interested in saving Station than trying to convince you of anything."

Teffinger nodded.

"Tell me about the other murders."

The woman retreated in thought—possibly deciding whether anything she said could be used against her?—and said, "I think I might know about three others, besides Alley Savannah. Like I said before, I don't think I was there in real time. I think he was thinking about them after the fact and that's what flashed over to me, visions in his memory."

"I understand."

"Okay, for one of them, there was a woman on the floor, laying face down on an oriental rug, a blond woman, youngish, early 20s or thereabouts, not moving, in an awkward position and looking very dead," she said.

"Did you see her face?"

"No, it was covered by her hair. I did see something else though. She had on black panties and that was all. So her back showed. She had a large tattoo back there."

"Of what?"

"I don't remember it that clearly," she said. "It was big and had a lot of color. It could have been a phoenix rising from the ashes, or possibly a dragon, something like that. Here's the funny part. Remember with Alley Savannah, where the guy wrote on a piece of paper? Well, he did the same thing here, only he didn't put it in the body."

"What'd he write?"

"If I recall right, it was the letters N O I Z."

"N O I Z?"

"Right."

"Okay."

"There was a whole wall filled with bookshelves and books," she said. "I actually think they were in a home library or study or something like that. Anyway, he reached up to the top shelf, pulled out a book, opened it, stuck the paper inside, and put the book back."

"What was the name of the book?"

"I didn't see a name."

"What color was it?"

"Red."

"A hardcover?"

"I think so. I don't recall it being flimsy."

She hesitated as if reaching for more and not getting it.

"What else do you remember?"

"Nothing," she said. "I'm surprised I remember that much to tell you the truth."

"Where were you when you had the vision?"

"Diving."

"Like before?"

"Yes."

"Same place?"

She nodded.

Teffinger looked around.

"N O I Z," he said. "If it's an acronym for something it's not one I'm familiar with."

"I Googled it and there's a Japanese cartoon rock band with that name," she said. "They supposedly play real energetic music. If that means something it's way beyond me."

"Maybe IZ means EYES," Teffinger said. "Same sound."

"So, no eyes?"

"Right."

Kovi-Ke's face tensed.

"Maybe she could see through his eyes the same way I can now," she said. "Maybe that's the reason he killed her.

No eyes—he didn't want someone else's eyes seeing through his."

"We're getting way ahead of ourselves."

She looked at him, deeply, and said, "I'm next."

"We don't know that."

"Maybe he's not after Station at all," she said. "Maybe he's just pretending to be after her to lure me here. No eyes then, no eyes now."

18

June 6
Friday Afternoon

The thought of Tarzan being close enough to bring down sent bark and bite into Teffinger's brain. It made him hop in the Tundra and point the front bumper towards the man's lair to see if he could figure out what was so important to risk a trip back to Denver. En route, he called Leigh Sandt, thanked her for tapping her CIA contact in Haiti, Poppy, and asked her for yet one more favor, namely to help him identify the back-tattoo victim, if indeed there was such a person.

"Hey, I have a good idea Mr. Nick-Man," she said.

"Like what?"

"Why don't I come to Denver and set up shop right at your desk so you don't have to bother with all these pesky little long-distance phone calls."

"Trust me," he said. "I know better than anyone that I wore my welcome out a long time ago. I'll make it up to you."

"How?"

"I don't know."

"When?"

"I don't know."

"Well, at least you're putting a lot of thought into it." She chuckled and said, "Blond, big tattoo, black panties, Oriental rug. I'll see what I can find out."

"Thanks."

"I'm also going to figure out what you can do to pay me back. I'll let you know what it is."

He smiled.

"Any chance it will involve Little Nicky?"

"None."

"I didn't think so."

He hung up and called Station to make sure she was okay and keeping her security guys close. She was; still reporting for work and sleeping at her loft, but otherwise laying low exactly as Teffinger suggested. She said, "When this is over, I want you to take me out and get me drunk, okay?"

"Absolutely."

"Promise?"

"Promise."

Tarzan's place was huge, four stories and filled with shadows, not to mention it had long ago been thoroughly combed by both Denver forensics and the FBI. Finding something new would be problematic at best, unless Tarzan had left fresh scratches. Armed with a 4-battery flashlight, Teffinger set to work starting on the top floor, looking for ductwork that had been cut open, cinderblocks that had been chiseled out, or whatever.

The going was slow.

Then it got slower.

Then it stopped.

Nothing showed up; not a single little iota of anything.

It could be that he was just missing it. It could also be that Tarzan didn't come back to Denver for anything tangible. He came back for Station and decided to taunt Teffinger in the process.

His phone rang and Kovi-Ke's voice came through, sounding like she just stepped off a roller coaster. "Nick, he left Denver. He's heading west, driving on an interstate, I-70 I think."

"How do you know?"

"His eyes. I had a flash. He's given up on Station. He's going after someone new."

"Who?"

"I don't know that, or where," she said. "From what I figure, he spotted you or me or both of us on his tail—probably me. Plus, Station was suddenly running around glued to two bodyguards. He knew something was up and decided to cut his losses."

Teffinger's blood raced.

"Where are you? I'll pick you up," he said.

"I'm driving. I'm out of Denver."

"Tell me you're not chasing him."

Silence.

Then she said, "You take care of yourself, Nick."

The line died.

He dialed back.

She didn't answer.

He threw a stray piece of rebar against the wall with every ounce of strength in his body. It landed with a dull thud and dropped unceremoniously to the floor.

19

June 6
Friday Afternoon

Against all better judgment, Teffinger worked the Tundra over to I-70 and headed west into the ever-elevating and looming Rockies, not calling anybody, not yet, not until he gave himself a chance to come to his senses and get his posterior back to Denver where it belonged.

His senses didn't come.

He called Sydney.

"I'm pretty sure Kovi-Ke rented a car, maybe earlier but probably sometime today. Find out from where. Get the make and model and license number and find out if it has a GPS. If it does, I want to know where it's at, and I want to be able to track it in real time."

"Why?"

"She bolted," he said. "She's heading west out of Denver."

"Why?"

"She's following the killer."

Sydney snickered.

"In that case she's following herself," she said. "She was feeling your heat and decided to cut her loses. Either that or she's luring you out of Denver so that Tarzan can do whatever it is that he's got planned."

Teffinger didn't disagree.

The thoughts had already been ricocheting like a diseased bullet inside his skull.

"The GPS," he said. "That's critical. Call me the second you have something."

The miles clicked off.

The mountains got bolder, taller, steeper, more rugged, more able to kill anyone who ventured off the trodden path. Traffic thinned and turned into a rhythm of swinging around 18-wheelers and RVs. He kept the radio off; not wanting to miss a single sane thought that might stray into his brain.

Every five minutes he dialed Kovi-Ke.

Every five minutes she didn't answer.

Then his phone rang.

He expected her voice but got a different one, one that belonged to the Haiti agent, Poppy. "I don't have much so far but I have a little," she said. "The voodoo night was real and, even as things like that go, brutal. Three women were abducted that night. They were targeted at Karnaval. Someone was passing out free bottled water. The ones they got were spiked. Kovi-Ke was the only one to make it out alive. The other two were sacrificed."

"Killed?"

"Yes," she said.

"So why not Kovi-Ke?"

"Unknown."

"Who orchestrated it?"

"Again unknown," she said. "I'm getting the information from people who know people who know people. When the question comes up as to who was behind it all, that's when things get real quiet. Either people don't know or are afraid to say. I'm going to keep digging but the easy part's over and, to tell you the truth, it might all be over."

"Don't give up."

"Never have but I'm also a realist," she said. "I'll be in touch either way."

He passed Idaho Springs and Georgetown, made a pit stop at the restrooms at Vail Pass, and charged farther West, past Vail and ever closer to Grand Junction and the western slope, looking into every car he came upon in hopes that Kovi-Ke was behind the wheel.

She never was.

The FBI profiler called.

"Back tattoo and black panties," she said. "They belong to Lachey Silk, age 25, murdered six months ago on January eighth, in New York City. Check your emails, I just sent you a photo of her. Ironically, she's your type; pretty, blond, the whole package. The detective in charge is a guy named Jack Canyon."

"No relation to Grand, I assume."

"No. Jack's a lot smaller. Here's his number—"

Teffinger checked his emails and opened the JPEG attachment. Leigh Sandt was right; the victim was his type, not that it had any relevance to anything.

Jack Canyon had a few interesting things to say when Teffinger called him. Lachey Silk, a fashion designer, a stunning little blond fashion designer to be precise, had been out clubbing the night she got murdered and had a lot of cocaine in her body to prove it. Her demise came by way of a knife to the heart, three times, abandoned in place on number three, apparently not needed for number four. There were the usual suspects—boyfriends, past and present, and girlfriends, past and present, and the people she'd been around earlier in the evening, plus someone she might have been blackmailing—but none were running to the front of the line.

"Tell me about the blackmail," Teffinger said.

"Wish I could. It was just a rumor," Canyon said. "The word was that she had something on someone and was getting money on the side. I was never able to get an angle on it though. Honestly, I don't know if it's true or not and probably never will."

"Tell me about the girlfriends."

"Not much to tell," Canyon said. "Just your basic hotties. A few of the priors had a little resentment but not to the level of murder, at least in my opinion."

"Any Jamaicans?"

"Not that I recall. We never went through the books, never had a reason to. So if the guy left a piece of paper in one of them we don't know about it."

"I understand. Can you run it down?"

"I don't know if they're still there or they've been thrown out or what but I'll check," Canyon said. "To be honest, you have my curiosity up. It says, NOIZ?"

"That's my understanding. It's in a red hardback on the top shelf."

Teffinger hung up and swung around a red Mustang. To his shock, Kovi-Ke was behind the wheel. She looked over, saw who he was, and floored it.

He got behind and dialed her.

She answered.

"Pull over," he said. "All I want to do is talk. Afterwards you're free to leave if you want."

"Is that the truth?"

"Yes," he said. "Pull over."

20

June 6
Friday Afternoon

Kovi-Ke pulled off at the first exit and was out of the car and at Teffinger's window before he came to a stop.

"Why are you following me?"

Teffinger got out, shut the door and leaned against it. "I'll answer that but before I do, let me say two words—Lachey Silk."

"Never heard of her."

"She's your black-panties tattoo girl," he said. "She was stabbed in the heart three times. It happened in New York six months ago, on January eighth."

"So she's real?"

"Was," Teffinger said. "Now she's a file."

Kovi-Ke frowned.

"Let me save you the trouble. Yes, I've been to New York before, but I wasn't there in January. I was home doing dives but, no, I probably can't prove it. No, I didn't know her; and no, I didn't kill her."

An 18-wheeler veered off the interstate and down the exit,

passing with squeaking brakes that smelled like hot bacon.

"She was pretty," Teffinger said. "She was also into girls, like Alley Savannah. She liked to party. Maybe you bumped into her at one point when you were in the city." He pulled his cell phone out and fumbled with it until he got what he wanted, a photo of a riveting blond, and kept his eyes on Kovi-Ke's face as he showed it to her. "This is her."

The woman looked.

A reaction registered on her face; fleeting, brief, quickly masked, but there nonetheless.

"I don't know her."

"Take a closer look."

She did and said, "I know her type. I've done her type, more than once, a lot more than once, actually. But I've never done her. I'd remember."

"You might have seen her, though? At a club or something?"

She shrugged.

"She's the kind I'd talk to, if that's what you're getting at."

"Okay."

"I didn't kill her," she said. "That's the bottom line so stop getting hung up in all kinds of little things that don't mean anything." She paused and added, "Is this why you followed me? To interrogate me about her?"

"No. I just found out about her ten minutes ago as a matter of fact."

"So why are you following me?"

He wrapped his arms around her and pulled her in.

"Why do you think?"

Then he kissed her.

She struggled, as if in the grip of the enemy, and then

softened in surrender.

His phone rang.

"Go ahead," Kovi-Ke said. "I have to use the facilities anyway. Teffinger watched the sway in her step as she disappeared into the pines and boulders and brush.

The FBI profiler was on the other end.

"Horrible news," she said. "Poppy's been murdered."

"Poppy in Haiti? That Poppy?"

"Yes."

"That can't be," Teffinger said. "I personally spoke to her not more than a hour ago."

"They cut her tongue off and gouged out her eyes," she said. "Most of her skin was off, as if she'd been dragged behind a car. Her body was dumped in an alley in downtown Port-au-Prince."

"That can't be."

"The CIA is on their way over to talk to me as we speak. You'll be next, so expect a knock on the door."

Teffinger slumped against the Tundra.

"She didn't want to get mixed up with voodoo. She told me that point blank. I put the pressure on her."

"Stop it," Leigh said. "I have to go. We'll talk later."

Teffinger's first thought was, Tarzan.

Tarzan did it.

The more he processed it though the less it fit. Tarzan was brutal but he wasn't the type to mutilate someone's face. No, this wasn't Tarzan's work. That didn't mean he wasn't involved somehow, it just meant that he personally didn't get the woman's blood on his hands.

Kovi-Ke came into sight with a spring in her step, a spring that fell away when she saw the look on his face. "What's wrong?"

He told her about how he'd hooked up with a CIA agent in Haiti to find the source of the voodoo night, working on the assumption that the source killed Alley Savannah and Lachey Silk, plus did whatever that was done that he didn't know about yet.

"She was just murdered, brutally, as an example." He kicked a rock. "I don't want you out chasing anyone. Come back to Denver."

She tightened her brow.

"You know I can't do that."

"Look, you're in a better position there," he said. "Right now you're just moving blind. You don't know where the guy is, you don't know where he's going, and you don't know where you're going. Sure, you might get lucky and end up in the same vicinity as him. But then what? You wouldn't even recognize him if he came up and asked you for directions. Come back to Denver and wait for a vision that lets you know where he is. Then you can fly there. It'll be quicker than driving there from whatever back-road sticks you might be in otherwise. Plus, if we're both in Denver, I can fly out with you."

She considered it.

"Thanks for the offer. I have to keep going, though."

Teffinger grabbed her elbow.

"Kovi-Ke."

"You said you wanted to talk and that I was free to leave afterwards," she said. "We talked. Now it's time for you to keep your promise."

Teffinger relaxed his grip and let his hand fall.

"Okay, then. I'll come with you."

She shook her head.

"You're a red flag. He knows you. I have to sneak up on him. To do that I have to be alone."

"That's crazy."

"Well, if that's crazy, then try this. I don't want you involved because I don't want you getting killed. There, better?"

She got in her car without looking back.

Then she was gone.

21

June 6
Friday Afternoon

Teffinger watched Kovi-Ke drive off, not knowing whether to follow her where she could see him, follow her from a mile back where she didn't know he was there, forget all about her and head back to Denver, or whatever. Then what he needed to do came to him. He dialed her, not expecting an answer but glad when it came, and said, "I'm going to Haiti."

"What for?"

"Answers, revenge, whatever's there. Someone in Haiti knows who the guy is."

"You're not serious."

"I just wanted you to know."

He hung up, got in the Tundra and pointed the front end east, back towards Denver.

His phone rang.

It was Kovi-Ke.

He didn't answer.

She might want to come with him. He didn't want to have to decide whether to let her or not. She called three more times. He didn't answer three more times.

Then the phone got silent.

He drove home where he got his passport and packed a suitcase, questioned his sanity one final time, and then headed to Denver International Airport where he found out the best travel route was through Miami. He bought a ticket, strapped himself into an aisle seat and gripped the armrests with sweaty palms as the city-sized hunk of metal raced down the runway and tried to muscle its way into the sky.

The wheels left the pavement.

The vibration stopped.

The woman next to him tapped his arm and said, "Are you okay?"

He looked over.

"Yeah, no worries. They'll be serving beer, don't you think?"

"Yeah, I guess."

"Good."

Late night, slightly tipsy, Teffinger landed in Miami, got a hotel room until morning, and then boarded a mid-sized jet to Haiti, surprised that he was actually doing what he was doing.

Unlike the flight to Miami, this one wasn't a can of sardines. The skies were crystal blue and drama-free. He'd only have to put up with them for a few short hours. Halfway there one of the flight attendants slipped into the seat next to him and said, "I've seen you somewhere before."

She was nice, his type, as nice as Kovi-Ke if the truth be told, but not someone he recognized or knew.

"I'm not from these parts," he said.

"How long will you be in Haiti?"

He shrugged.

"I don't know. A day or two, maybe a week, it's all up in the air."

"Your eyes are two different colors."

"That's true."

"Now I know where I know you from. GQ, you were on the cover. At least I think that was you. Was it?"

He nodded.

"I think they picked me because of my eyes," he said.

"Well, they chose good." She wrote digits on a napkin. "That's my number. I'll be in town for three days before I have to fly out again. Call me and we'll do something. I'll show you all the haunts."

Teffinger almost shoved the paper in his pocket.

Instead he handed it back.

"I'm here on business," he said. "It might get a little rough."

She ran a finger down his hand and said, "I like it rough."

"Not this rough."

She shoved the napkin in his shirt pocket, patted his chest and said, "If you change your mind."

Then she was gone, wiggling up the aisle.

Teffinger took the paper out and studied it, deciding. She'd be a crazy little thing in bed. He had no formal commitments to Kovi-Ke. Then he frowned. He'd probably have withdrawal pains later, but he ripped the napkin to pieces before he could think about it any more.

Right now he was a disease.

There was no use infecting innocent people.

Mid-morning, the flight touched down uneventfully at Port-au-Prince International Airport. Teffinger made his way through customs one painful second at a time and then hopped in a cab and said, "Villa Sky."

That's where Kovi-Ke stayed when she was abducted.

As the cab pulled off, a knock came at the window.

The driver braked.

The door opened and the stewardess hopped in, a smile coming to her face from the look on Teffinger's. She said to the driver, "Toussaint, take me home."

"Sure thing, pretty lady. You're second."

"Actually I'm first," she said. "He's going where I'm going."

The driver gave Teffinger a look.

Then he did a one-eighty and took off.

DAY FOUR

June 7
Saturday

22

June 7
Saturday Morning

The stewardess—Modeste—ended up squashed against Teffinger as the cab driver picked up three more passengers en route. The pressure of her thigh against his went straight to his brain, so much so that he could even tolerate the cramped quarters.

They got closer and closer to a mountainside of colored structures that all seemed attached to one another. From a distance they seemed bright and inviting. Up close they took on a more deprived and dangerous patina.

The driver dropped them as far up as the road allowed.

Modeste grabbed Teffinger's hand and said, "Don't be afraid."

Then they headed up, winding through stairs and alleys for some time before finally entering an aqua green three-story structure, something in the nature of an apartment building sandwiched between more of the same. A dark stairwell took them to the top floor, where a short hallway ended with a door on each side. Modeste slipped a key into the door on the right and found the lock jimmied. The knob turned and she entered.

Then she gasped.

Teffinger stepped in and saw why.

The place was trashed.

"This is getting more and more frequent," she said.

"It's happened before?"

"Too many times," she said. "They're looking for drugs or guns or money or whatever is worth anything. Liquor, anything like that. Too bad for them I don't have anything."

"So you're not in trouble or anything? No one came here to get you?"

"No."

"Well, that's good."

"Yeah, my lucky day."

Teffinger helped her straighten up.

A million years of recessed caveman genetics made his peripheral vision size her up at every opportunity. Her skin was dark; her body was compelling; and the way she moved, well, that was the best of it all. Every stance was a pose; every change of position was a song. Her mouth was cute and wide and given to easy smiles.

His phone rang and Sydney's voice came through. "Kovi-Ke's back in Denver. She said she had another flash, from Denver. The guy had doubled back. She's back here trying to find him, just like before. I'll be honest, Teff, I have no idea what to make of her. She's here, she's there, she seems legit when you talk to her face to face, but how can she be?"

"Call Station," he said. "Tell her to keep her guard up. Don't let her get relaxed just because nothing visible is showing on her radar screen. Has there been any sign of Tarzan?"

"Nothing, not a peep. The CIA guys were peeping, though.

They went to the chief when they found out you weren't in town. They gave him an earful. He took it but he's saving it up for you. It's in a box with your name on it."

"You didn't tell him where I went, did you?"

"No. I only said you were on vacation."

"Which I am."

"Do you want my advice?"

"No."

"Good, because here it is," she said. "Get your posterior back to Denver, get the CIA behind you and figure out what Kovi-Ke is up to."

"I will, I will and I will. Until I do, though, get close to Kovi-Ke, but be seriously careful. Make sure she doesn't kill Station; and make sure no one kills her. Most importantly, make sure no one kills you. Oh, one more thing. Kovi-Ke said she thought the guy did four murders. She only gave me the stories on two of them, Alley Savannah and Lachey Silk. Get the other two and run them to ground. Don't go through Leigh Sandt, though. I'm sure she's buying GQs by the dozens as we speak just so she can shred the covers."

"Good visual."

"Thanks."

"I think I'll go out and buy some while I can, for when you give me those same moments in the future."

He smiled.

"Good idea."

"Where can I get a shredder sharpened? Do you know?"

He hung up, turned to Modeste and said, "What do you know about voodoo?"

Her face tightened.

"I know that it's not for tourists. I know that it's not a

plaything."

"Who in town practices it so hard that they kill people?"

Her eyes retreated in fear.

"Even asking that question is a dangerous thing."

"Maybe," he said. "But so is not asking it."

He told her about Kovi-Ke's abduction during Karnaval, the fact that she could now see through a killer's eyes, and the reason he was in Haiti, namely to get to the source of the night in question.

At the end Modeste said, "This woman, Kovi-Ke. It sounds like you've fallen for her. Am I right?"

It was a good question, one he'd avoided asking himself.

"The whole thing's volatile," he said. "To be honest she's like a loaded gun. I'm never sure if she's pointed at me or away."

"Either way, you and me are not going to have sex, are we?"

Teffinger hated to give the answer.

He hated to lock out the possibility.

But there was only one answer to give.

"No."

Modeste turned and shook her backside at him, a tribute to what he was missing.

"Tell her she's a lucky girl, this Kovi-Ke." She grew serious and added, "The person you're looking for is a voodoo woman named Janjak. She's twice the devil and then some. My advice is to leave right now and forget you ever heard her name, which by the way, you didn't hear from me."

23

June 7
Saturday Morning

Modeste said, "Janjak can steal your soul from a distance and you wouldn't even know it until she started to carve it up with a razorblade. She can break you from the inside just because it amuses her. Death is no escape. In fact, when you die it gets worse. At least while you're alive you have worldly elements in your life. In death there's nothing except Janjak. Once she has you, she has you forever."

Teffinger walked to the window and peeked out.

He saw a little girl with tattered clothes pushing a two-wheeled bike that was too big for her. Her face and arms glistened with sweat. The sun played off a pink bow in her hair.

"Where can I find her?"

"You're not hearing what I'm saying," Modeste said.

"No one will ever know," he said. "I promise."

Modeste shook her head.

"It's for your own good," she said. "Don't be angry with me."

Teffinger took another look outside.

The little girl was gone.

An old man appeared from around a corner, hunched over from the weight of too many decades. Behind him, two men came into view, walking briskly past the old man to across the way and then looking up at Modeste's apartment. The one in the red shirt looked like he could kill every living thing on the planet and not even blink. Teffinger dropped back, motioned Modeste over to the edge of the window and said, "Friends of yours?"

Her face contorted.

She grabbed her purse and said, "Come on!"

Ten seconds later they were out the back bedroom window and bounding down a rusty fire escape.

A safe distance away, increasing that distance with every passing second and continuously looking over his shoulder, Teffinger said, "Who are they?"

"I don't know."

He stopped and grabbed her elbow.

"Are you going to tell me what's going on or not?"

She broke free and kept going.

"No."

He caught up.

"You didn't bring me home because you liked me. You brought me for protection."

"I brought you home for both," she said. "I was going to give you sex either way, if it makes you feel any better."

"It doesn't."

He didn't really care.

His suitcase was back at her place but his wallet and passport and cell phone were in his back pockets. There was nothing in the suitcase that he couldn't live without or anything inside that could identify him. No, wait, there was—his plane ticket. It was one-way, he didn't really need it any more, but it had his name on it.

A high-revving motorcycle made Teffinger twist his head around. It was the two pit bulls, closing fast from behind, fixated on their targets. The one in back—the one with the red shirt—had a gun, trying to finalize his aim. Teffinger jerked Modeste behind a parked van just as the shot came. It passed so close that it actually flicked his hair.

The brakes locked and the wheels squealed to a stop.

"Run!" Teffinger said.

Modeste stared at him, frozen.

"Run I said!"

She started but slowly.

"Go!"

She turned and ran with all her might.

The bike was down, stopping too fast to control, and grinding to a stop on its side a hundred feet away. The two men muscled their bodies off the ground and turned in his direction. The passenger who shot at him, the one in the red shirt, had the gun back in hand now, gripped in a steel fist as he approached. The other one had a large knife, black and worn. A serrated edge flashed for just a second as the sun caught it.

There was nowhere for Teffinger to run.

They were too close.

A shot came, louder than thunder and ripping through the van's back panel with a terrible sound.

Teffinger's heart raced.

He spotted a broken bottle at his feet and snatched it up.

Then, as they got close enough, Teffinger swung around the edge of the van and whipped the bottle at the red shirt with every ounce of strength in his body.

The man flinched at the last second but not fast enough.

His finger pulled the trigger.

A bullet ricocheted.

The glass landed squarely in his face jags first and stuck.

Blood splattered.

A frantic hand reached up to pull it out but stopped working halfway up. The man fell to the ground with the bottle still in his face, twitched for a second and then stopped moving.

The other man dived for the gun.

Teffinger got a foot to it first and kicked it away.

The man squared off, waving the knife back and forth with a deadly intensity.

Then he turned and ran.

Teffinger didn't chase him.

He watched as the man got to the bike, fired it up and fishtailed the back tire as he squealed off. He threw one wild look over his shoulder as he twisted the throttle and then he was gone.

Teffinger gave the red shirt one final glance.

The man's eyes were open, staring at nothing.

A fly landed on his nose and twisted in a little dance.

Across the street, a few gathered faces watched.

Against his better judgment, or maybe because of it, Teffinger searched the man's pockets and was glad he did. There he found a wallet that might have identification, but more importantly he found his own plane ticket, the one that had been in the suitcase back in Modeste's apartment.

That would have tied him to the scene.

He also found money and keys.

He tossed the money on the ground, stuffed everything else in his pocket and ran off in the direction Modeste had gone.

24

June 7
Saturday Afternoon

In his mind, Teffinger did nothing wrong. He'd acted in self-defense and, if it had happened in the states, he would have stayed at the scene and let the justice system run its short and understanding course. Here though he didn't know the laws, or how much they might be ignored or twisted or distorted in the name of corruption or extortion, nor did he know who the dead man was, or who he might be connected to that might be able to pull ugly strings.

So he left.

For better or worse, he left.

With any luck there'd been no security cameras in the area, the few faces across the street either didn't get much of a look or knew better than to get involved, and the police investigation, if even there was one, would die a sudden and final death.

He wandered the streets of Port-au-Prince, hoping to have enough luck left to stumble onto Modeste. He saw her once but it turned out to not be her, instead being a woman who made eye contact and let a smile briefly cross her face before turning away.

Police sirens echoed through the streets with increasingly regularity.

Teffinger didn't like them.

He found a bar, wedged himself into a dark corner and sipped lukewarm beer.

The dead man was someone named Widson Danticat, who had an address that Teffinger pulled up on Google Earth, to discover that it wasn't that far away, half an hour or so on foot, a little longer if the heat got to him.

He swallowed what was left of his beer, left a good tip and headed that way.

Outside, he got his bearings, and then headed back in.

The guy behind the bar was an older man in a stained wife-beater shirt who talked to guys on stools in French.

Teffinger leaned on the counter and said, "I'm supposed to meet a friend named Janjak this afternoon but I lost her address. You wouldn't know her by any chance, would you?"

The man's face tightened.

"No."

Teffinger nodded.

"It was a long shot."

Then he left.

Danticat's apartment was a mess, not ransacked, just the by-product of someone who placed no value on order and neatness. Dirty dishes filled the sink, tattered sheets hung as window coverings and stuff was everywhere—not good stuff, not useful stuff or even potentially useful stuff at some point in the future. No, this was stuff that should have been kicked to the curb decades ago.

The walls were too close.

The ceiling was too low.

The windows were too small.

It was worse than an elevator jammed up with snakes.

Teffinger's instinct was to get the hell out of there before some incurable disease jumped on him but instead he dug in, looking for anything that might explain why the guy had been after Modeste.

Clearly Danticat wasn't self-motivated.

He didn't have the drive to tend to his own existence, let alone be focused and involved enough to kill someone out of his own desires.

He was working for someone else.

That's where his motivation came from, no doubt in the form of money.

That wasn't good.

That meant Modeste was still in as much danger as she was before. There would be a thousand other Danticat's in the city to replace this one with.

One thing about the guy, he liked his music. He had an actual CD player and three shelves of CDs. An open case on top of the player said *Aitch-M – Closer to Nowhere* on red lettering over a gray background that, on closer look, depicted a gargoyle flying over an evil city with a half-naked woman clutched in its talons. Teffinger leafed through a few CDs on the shelf and found them equally unknown and obscure.

Come on.

Who hired you?

An old VHS player was wired into an equally old boxy TV, not a flat screen by any stretch. For grins, Teffinger fired them up.

What he saw he could hardly believe.

He popped the tape out, gripped it like it was life itself, and got the hell out of there.

25

25

June 7
Saturday Afternoon

Teffinger headed to Modeste's apartment on the chance she'd returned, to find her huddled behind closed curtains, surprised beyond logic to find him showing up alive, but equally as ecstatic, which she proved by gripping him in a tight full-body hug and softly trembling with her head on his chest. He told her what happened after she ran off—how he'd killed the man in the red shirt, took his wallet, left the scene and then broke into the guy's apartment.

"This," he said tapping the videotape, "was in the guy's apartment. I only watched a little of it but it's a voodoo scene."

"Voodoo?"

He nodded.

"We need to get to a player. I want to see what happens and I want you to tell me if Janjak is in it." He paused and added, "Mister Red Shirt was someone for hire. That means he'll be replaced and my guess is sooner than later. Grab whatever you need from here. We're not coming back."

Two minutes later they were down the fire escape and leaving the vicinity.

"You're mixed up in voodoo," Teffinger said. "Tell me what's going on. Who's after you and why?"

She shook her head.

"There's no voodoo," she said. "Have you ever heard of the rock group Her? They're from England."

"No."

"Well, the front man for that group is a guy named Johnnie Rail. Does that name ring a bell?"

"No."

"Well, Rail has a seaside villa here in Haiti," she said. "A couple of months ago, during a flight, a pretty young woman named May-May struck up a conversation with me. It turns out she was Her's manager. We hit it off pretty good; she liked me, and ended up offering me a job as her assistant, right there on the spot. She needed someone as an interface for anything Haiti related, someone who knew the lay of the land. But when Rail wasn't here in Haiti, which would be most of the time, I would be on tour with the band."

"Sounds fun."

"That's what I thought," she said. "But I really don't know anything about the music industry and had a suspicion that I wouldn't be able to earn my keep. I pictured myself getting fired. So I told her thanks but no thanks."

"Personally I would have taken it," Teffinger said. "Unless the group is a bunch of holes."

"I don't know if they are or not, but May-May said if I ever changed my mind, just stop by the villa. It was a standing invitation."

"Do it now," Teffinger said. "It'll get you out of Haiti."

She frowned.

"Unfortunately, something happened."

Teffinger glanced over his shoulder. Walking thirty steps behind them was a man in a white T who looked like a fighter.

"So what happened?" he said.

"One day about a month ago when I was coming back from a flight I saw May-May across the terminal," she said. "She was out the door and in a cab before I could get to her, but I knew she was in town. Seeing her made me reflect on my decision. I figured I'd been cutting myself too short. If I tried, I could make it in any business, including the music industry."

"I believe that."

"So that afternoon I went over to the villa," she said. "No one knew I was going. When I got there I found five dead bodies."

"Really?"

"Really," she said. "There were four dead men and May-May, she was there dead too. From what I could figure out, two locals came to rob the place. They almost made it out before getting discovered. There was a shootout and everyone ended up dead, two guys from the villa, the two robbers and May-May. Next to one of the robber's bodies were two large black bags with leather handles, sort of like a doctor's bag, only bigger. I shouldn't have done what I did, but I opened one of them up. Inside were bars of gold. I took both bags and left. I shouldn't have done it but they were right there in my hands. No one knew I'd been there. I figured that they would think there had been three robbers and that the third one made off with the stuff."

Teffinger shook his head.

"That was a mistake."

"Yeah, I know," she said. "When I got home I found a small leather case at the bottom of one of the bags, about the size of a book. Inside that case were six leather pouches that had old American movie star names on them."

"Movie stars?"

She nodded.

"Marilyn Monroe, Sophia Loren, Ava Gardner, Jean Harlow, Rita Hayworth and Lauren Bacall. Each of the pouches had a very large diamond inside."

"So you had gold and diamonds—"

"Yes. Months went by and everything was silent. No one came my way looking for anything. Then, on my latest flight, my friend Constance, who checks my apartment for me every now and then when I'm gone, called and said the place had been broken into. She thought it was just the usual, mostly because the food had also been taken. Still, I was a little nervous and brought you home for protection, just in case. When we got there, I was 99% sure it was just the usual locals looking for whatever they could steal. Then those two men showed up outside and I knew that someone had somehow traced things to me."

"So you think they work for Johnnie Rail? He's trying to get his stuff back?"

She nodded.

"That would be my best guess," she said. "On the other hand, they could be associated with the robbers. There's one more possibility. They could be with the police, if Rail made a police report as to anything missing. I'm not sure if he did or not. The coins might be black market stuff so he might not have mentioned them. But they might be legitimate and now the police are looking for them on the side, for their own little retirement plan, not to return to Rail."

"So where's all this stuff now?"

"The bars, I cut up and sold in New York," she said. "I put the money—just over a million, actually—in a bank account in the Caymans."

"What about the movie stars?"

"I still have them; Constance is storing them for me at her place. I don't know how to sell them and was afraid to start asking questions."

Teffinger exhaled.

"When you sold the bars, that's how your involvement got back to Johnnie Rail. That's a lot of gold to liquidate. Give him back all the money you got, that's my advice. Give him the movie stars too."

"I can't."

"Why not?"

"Because the money's in a safe bank account in my name," she said. "Do you have any idea how that feels? Besides, Johnnie Rail doesn't need it. He's doing just fine without it."

"I'll bet he'd disagree."

"Maybe, but I don't care," she said. "I'm taking the first flight out of here in the morning and I'm never coming back. I'm the world's newest ghost. I'm gone, disappeared, vanished."

"He'll find you, sooner or later he'll find you."

"That's a chance I'm willing to take."

Teffinger glanced over his shoulder.

The guy in the white T was still back there. Another man was with him now. They looked intense, as if they were about to bite a rattlesnake.

26

June 7
Saturday Afternoon

Teffinger didn't wait long to check the two guys behind him again, five seconds or thereabouts, maybe less. To his astonishment they had closed the gap with an absolute silence and were now two deadly shapes right behind him. A powerfully cocked fist immediately landed at the back of his head with the impact of a brick. Colors exploded inside his skull and his body staggered briefly before crashing down. Everything turned black before he hit the ground.

At some point he regained consciousness.

At first he didn't know where he was or what had happened. His head felt as if a little demon had gotten stuck inside and was trying to bust out with a ball peen hammer.

His neck was whiplashed.

His throat was dry.

"Modeste!"

He struggled to his feet and swung his eyes to the left, right, behind him, up the street, everywhere.

She was nowhere.

She was gone.

The two men were equally gone.

He noticed something on the ground, at first foreign and then as the videotape from the shooter's apartment; the voodoo scene.

He picked it up and staggered away.

It took a while for his head to clear and for options to materialize. It was a given that the two men took Modeste on behalf of someone, probably Johnnie Rail, but possibly the initial robbers or the police.

They would make her talk.

They'd hold her and keep her alive until they got the money she stashed in the Caymans, plus the movie stars, which were in the custody of Modeste's friend, Constance, whoever that was.

Then what?

Would they kill her?

Would they kill Constance too?

More importantly, why should Teffinger care? He had no dog in the fight. Modeste had done nothing but play him from the start, first by bringing him home for protection without any apparent care as to the risk to him, and then initially denying what she'd done. She'd also ignored Teffinger's advice to give everything back, although, in hindsight, she'd been captured before she could have done that even if she wanted to.

So why should Teffinger help her?

She'd gotten herself into this mess.

She'd done nothing but play him for her own greedy gain.

He kicked a pop can.

All the logic wasn't helping.

He couldn't talk himself out of doing what he was going to do.

He turned around and headed back to Modeste's place, entered from the fire escape and then searched for signs of Constance's identity; a photo, letter, anything however small that might indicate who she was.

The midday heat wrapped around him with the strength of a python.

The place had no cross ventilation.

He turned on two small fans that did nothing other than mock him with their own inefficiency.

Nothing useful showed up.

Whoever Constance was, she was determined to remain invisible.

He took a cold shower

The water was life itself, filling his pores with all things good.

Suddenly the curtain pulled open.

A woman stood there, a white woman, startled to see him.

"Constance?"

She stepped back.

Then she ran.

He got to her before she could get to the door, flipped her to the carpet and pinned her down.

"I'm not going to hurt you," he said. "I'm a friend of Modeste. By extension, that makes me your friend too. They took Modeste."

"Who took Modeste? Where is she?"

"Johnnie Rail's people, I'm assuming," he said. "You're

next once they find out you have the diamonds. I need you to give them to me so I can use them as a bargaining chip to get her back."

"Get off me."

He complied.

Then he headed back to the bathroom and said, "I'm going to dry off and get dressed. Don't go anywhere."

He kicked the bathroom door shut with his foot.

The water was still running.

He stepped back in.

He needed more of it.

He needed a lot more.

Everything else was secondary.

When he got out five minutes later, the apartment was empty.

The woman was gone.

27

June 7
Saturday Afternoon

Teffinger took a place on the couch and focused on the ball peen hammers inside his head. He'd been hit before, more than his fair share, but this was different. He closed his eyes. A moment later he slumped into a laying position.

He cursed his weakness.

It did no good.

His thoughts got tangled up in strange conspiracy theories and voodoo ghosts.

Then everything turned black.

He slept.

On and on and on he slept.

He slept until the jet lag and the commotion and the fighting and the intensity of the last few days all got refilled. Then he slept longer.

It was then that a strange coolness washed over him.

He opened his eyes to find Constance dabbing a wet washcloth on his face. He focused on her eyes and liked them; partly because they were green—his favorite color—

but mostly because he could see into them. He could see the inside of her. That didn't work with all eyes. It did with hers.

He muscled into a sitting position.

The demons inside his head still worked their hammers, albeit not as fiercely, but not to be ignored either. Constance saw the expression on his face, fumbled in her purse and came out with three pills, which Teffinger swallowed without water or asking what they were. Based on the woman's eyes, they were something good.

"I'm glad you didn't leave," Constance said. "I was afraid you did."

Teffinger stretched.

"Why'd you come back?"

She handed him a small leather case.

Teffinger opened it up, and found the six leather pouches exactly as Modeste had described, with one exception. One was empty.

"Where's Marilyn?"

"I'm going to hang onto her," Constance said.

Teffinger frowned.

"Bad idea. She'll get you killed."

Constance exhaled.

"She's a final bargaining chip, in case you get killed or taken," she said.

Teffinger got up and looked outside.

The harsh tension of everyday struggles lay over the land.

"Do you know who Madonna is?" he said.

"You mean the singer?"

"Yeah, her."

"Sure, who doesn't?"

"You remind me of her a little bit," he said. "The way she

looked in her Like a Virgin video."

"Never saw it."

"It was before your time. We better go."

28

June 7
Saturday Evening

The Like a Virgin pretty, Constance, had some valid points, namely she knew the lay of the land, plus Modeste was her friend, meaning she could help Teffinger dial up an exchange with Johnnie Rail. Teffinger wasn't interested in putting her in harm's way and frowned to prove it. To prove it even more, he took her to the airport, made her promise not to come back until he personally called her and said it was safe, put her on a plane and didn't leave until she pulled into the sky. Then he rented a ratty straight-handlebar motorcycle at a dubious place near the airport that charged him more than the sign said, drove to Constance's apartment and entered, compliments of her key and permission.

The place hadn't been ransacked.

He pulled the curtains shut, closing out a twilight sky, and found a well-stocked fridge. He was making a yogurt and cucumber sandwich when his phone rang and Sydney's voice came through.

"Have you heard what happened?"

He braced.

"No."

"We had a murder," she said. "A woman. It was pretty brutal."

"Station?"

"No. We're still trying to identify the body. Here's what makes it interesting. Her body was down at BNSF, a stone's throw from Tarzan's place."

"Tarzan—"

"A couple of the switching guys found her about twenty minutes ago. I'm at the scene right now. She's naked. Her throat was slit. Here's the most interesting part—her eyes were gouged out. All hell's breaking loose down here."

Teffinger pictured it.

"Did you find a note?"

"What do you mean?"

"A note, you know, the kind of thing that was left with those girls in Miami and New York," he said.

"No, nothing like that. You think it's the same guy?"

"Yeah, maybe. I don't know. Search around. Check her body cavities. If it's not there, go out in an ever-increasing radius. Don't stop until you've exhausted every inch. I don't care if you have to go a hundred yards. Check every boxcar, including the roofs. Check inside Tarzan's place too."

"Okay. By the way, the chief has a message for you. Get your ass back here, right now."

"He's so poetic. Tell him Robert Frost has nothing on him."

He finished making the sandwich and sat on the couch, chomping into it and washing it down with orange juice straight out of the carton. The new murder played inside his head like a bad 8mm film. He could see the knife ripping across the throat. He could see the blood spurting out of the gaping hole. He could see the look of horror on her face. He could see her spent body on the ground, only seconds dead, while someone—Tarzan?—worked at getting her eyes out, which wasn't as easy as it sounded.

Tarzan, is that you?

Are you sending me a message?

Suddenly his phone rang. He expected Sydney, or maybe the chief, but the voice that came through belonged to Jack Canyon, the detective in charge of Lachey Silk's murder. "Red book, top shelf," Canyon said. "We ran it down."

"What'd you find?"

"Well, after the murder, the landlord ended up putting a lien on everything in the apartment for unpaid rent," he said. "All the books got boxed up, with a lot of other stuff, and placed in a large locked storage bin down in the guts of the building. It's all been under lock and key almost since day one. He let us in and we dug through one dusty box after another. We finally found it, a red hardcover. Inside was the piece of paper, exactly as you said. NOIZ."

"So it actually exists—"

"It does," he said. "There were no prints on the paper but a lot on the book. We're running them but no one of interest has popped up yet. That book could have been handled or read by twenty different people."

"Well, let me know."

"The thing that is of interest, though, is that the book's been in storage all this time," he said. "You could tell that not only from the landlord's story but also from the way the boxes were laying undisturbed and uniformly covered in dust. This particular box was underneath several others and way in the back. To me, that means that this isn't some after-the-fact prank or anything like that."

"It was put there by the killer," Teffinger said. "That's what you're saying."

"That's exactly what I'm saying."

Teffinger took a swallow of orange juice and said, "I'm leaning towards NOIZ as standing for no eyes. We had a homicide in Denver today where the victim's eyes were gouged out. I believe it was the same guy who did the deed on Lachey Silk. He thinks that people can see through his eyes and that's why he kills them, to get free."

"That's a weird theory."

"It's a weird world," Teffinger said. "You're the man, for running that down so good. I'll be in touch."

He took a peek outside, found everything normal, and then went into the bedroom to see if there was a window facing the back. There wasn't but there was something just as good, an old videotape player under the bed.

He connected it to the TV and powered it up.

Come on, work.

The lights came on.

Yeah, that's the way.

He put the voodoo tape in—the one he got from the shooter's apartment, the guy who made Teffinger throw a broken bottle into his face—and punched play. A bizarre voodoo scene sprang to life, jerky, grainy, taken with a bad camera by a bad amateur at night. A woman, a white woman with blond hair, was bound spread-eagle on the ground. Wicked drums beat and frantic dancers gyrated. Another woman dangled a snake above her head, then lopped off the head with a machete and dripped the blood and guts into the victim's eyes and nose and mouth.

The camera zoomed in on the woman's face.

Teffinger's heart raced.

It looked like Station.

The scene ended with a jerk of the camera and then went black.

He replayed it all, this time focusing on the victim's face, trying to decide one way or the other if indeed it was Station. In the end he was 80% sure it was.

He wasn't positive, but pretty damn close.

29

June 7
Saturday Night

As twilight thickened over Haiti, Teffinger worked his way out of Port-au-Prince on the motorcycle until he was good and far from prying eyes. Where the road came close to a beach, he double-checked for dangers one final time, concluded he was as alone as he could ever be, and then buried the box of diamonds three feet under the sand near the tree-line in a location he carefully paced off from a trunk.

When he got back to the bike, there were still no signs of cars or humans.

He memorized the location and then continued up the broken dirt and gravel road, getting closer and closer to Johnnie Rail's villa. He had no specific plan other than to try to get a look at the place and figure out if Modeste was being held there.

The lights of the villa came into view a kilometer up ahead, peeking through thick tropical foliage. Teffinger killed the bike's lights and maneuvered it well off the road, out of sight of any headlights that might swing by.

There were no distinguishable markers, other than one rock near the edge of the road, no larger than a briefcase.

It was almost full dark.

He memorized the location as best he could and proceeded to close the gap on foot.

The villa sat in the sand at the edge of a circular lagoon, like the crown jewel in a ring. It pulsed with a loud reggae beat, barely audible at this distance but prominent at the source. A soft half-moon shimmied with an eerie translucence, more like a shadow than a light, dancing lightly on the water on quiet ghost feet. Teffinger made his way to where the trees met the sand and crept one careful foot after another towards the glowing yellow lights of the structure.

A party was in play, beating the tropical night with a live band next to the pool, throngs of scantily clad pretties both black and white, and lots and lots of voices, the kind that came out when too much booze or drugs went in.

Teffinger made his way to the closest shadows, assessed one more time the sanity of what he was about to do, and then strolled into sight towards the crowd like he owned the place. He pulled a beer out of a tub of ice, twisted the top off and took as long swallow.

Eyes fell on him.

He detected them in his peripheral vision.

He turned full on to find they belonged to a petite Asian woman with long black hair, a T ripped off just under her breasts, exposing a taut little tummy, and a short white wraparound that extended to mid-thigh. She didn't turn away when he looked at her. Instead she headed straight for him on bare feet, sipping from a glass as she came.

"I'm Evil Angel," she said. "I'm from Hong Kong."

The words were in English.

Teffinger took a swallow.

"You're a long way from home."

"Yes I am," she said.

"How'd you end up here?"

"Fate," she said. "Do you believe in fate?"

Teffinger nodded.

"Sometimes."

"How about right now?"

He shrugged.

"Maybe. Do you know Johnnie Rail?"

"Of course."

"Is he here?"

"Yes but we don't need him right now. What we need is a little privacy." She reached into his front pants pocket and wiggled her fingers. "Did you bring me any?"

"I probably did," he said. "But first I need to talk to Johnnie Rail." He headed into the crowd towards the open glass doors of the house and said over his shoulder, "I'll be back. Don't go anywhere."

"I won't."

Inside, he dropped to the lower level and searched for Modeste. She was nowhere. He made his way up, through the main floor, and then to the upper floor, interrupting lots of sex, but not feeling too badly about it. He headed back outside and fanned out, checking the outlying buildings and enclaves.

Modeste was nowhere.

Evil Angel had some news for him when he returned. "Did you catch Johnnie before he left?"

"He left?"

"Two minutes ago."

"To where?"

"I don't know."

"Do you have a car?"

"No. Johnnie's the one with all the cars."

"He has more than one?"

"A lot more than one."

He grabbed her hand.

"Show me."

Two minutes later they were in old rusty piece of crap Land Cruiser, 70s vintage, with no doors or top, busting speed down the pitch-black road. Evil Angel was in the passenger seat, impervious to Teffinger's repeated requests to stay behind.

A hundred yards into it, he slammed on the brakes.

"Check the back tire!"

"Why?"

"See if it's flat."

When she got out, he floored it and didn't look back.

Five minutes later red taillights appeared up ahead. Teffinger closed the gap with every ounce of power he could muster from the puny little 4-banger under the hood.

He pounded the horn.

It didn't work.

Then he rammed the taillights.

It wasn't hard, just enough to get the other vehicle to stop.

Then something happened that he didn't expect.

The other vehicle slammed on the brakes.

The Land Cruiser caught the bumper at a bad angle. It tilted sideways onto two wheels, twitched violently back and fourth as he tried to regain control, and then pitched into a death roll with all the fury of a screaming beast.

DAY FIVE

June 8
Sunday

30

June 8

Sunday Morning

Teffinger opened his eyes to find himself in a bed in a dark room in the middle of the night. Pale moonlight shined through balcony doors, enough to vaguely define a vaulted ceiling and silk window coverings swaying softly from an outside breeze.

Next to him, sleeping soundly on top of the covers, was a naked woman with long black hair. Teffinger couldn't make out the face but recognized the perfume.

It was Evil Angel.

Did he have sex with her?

He couldn't remember.

He remembered crashing the Land Cruiser; that was it, nothing afterwards. He slipped out of bed carefully so as to not wake the evil one, found he was wearing nothing, and headed for the bathroom.

A large gauze patch was taped to the side of his stomach. He peeled it open to find a wound five or six inches long, held closed with a large number of stitches and disinfected with something that made his skin a zinc color. He sealed the patch and then pressed against it. The wound itself responded with a deep pain but nothing resonated underneath it. It appeared to be a flesh wound with no deeper damage.

His throat was dried sandpaper.

He drank a full glass of water, rubbing it into the pores of his mouth with his tongue.

Then he drank another.

Several darkish bruises marked his body, together with three smaller bandages, all of which showed stitches underneath, but minor in scope.

His clothes hung over the shower rod.

Everything that should be in his pockets was, including his wallet, fully intact, and his cell phone, which did not appear to have been tampered with or used.

He turned the lights off, opened the door and made his way back to bed in the dark, slipping in quietly so as to not wake the evil one.

Every caveman gene in his body told him to take her; take her until she lost every semblance of control; take her so hard she'd never recover, not in a thousand cave-girl years.

He resisted the genes and let his thoughts turn to Kovi-Ke, the big question mark in his life, the reason he was here in Haiti trying to figure her out, or protect her, or arrest her, or whatever it was that the final answer would be.

What was she?

Who was she?

Why did he care?

Evil Angel breathed with a soft rhythm next to him.

All he needed to do was shake her shoulder. That's all it would take to enter heaven, the angel part of her. That's all it would take to bring out the gyrations of her body and the warmth of her mouth and the energy of all that little life inside her.

He closed his eyes but sleep didn't come.

He was going to be killed soon; maybe tomorrow, maybe not for a few days, but soon. He could feel it down in his gut. It was as real as the moon creeping into the room. All he hoped is that it wasn't at the hands of Kovi-Ke. That would be too much to handle. That would be too ironic of an ending. That would be too much of an ultimate mistake.

He fought with the ghosts in his head for some time before finally disappearing into a safe vortex where they couldn't follow.

31

June 8
Sunday Morning

Teffinger bolted upright in bed, covered in sweat, the victim of a horrific dream where Kovi-Ke slit his throat from behind and then walked off before he hit the floor, not even bothering to look back; he was that insignificant. Dawn had broken, not by much, but enough to wash the room in a warm Caribbean glow. He fell on his back, grateful that his death was only a dream.

Evil Angel opened an eye, rolled on her back and stretched her arms high above her head. Her Hong Kong skin was golden brown.

Her body was perfect.

Her nipples were candy.

She rolled over, draped a leg over him and got her face close. "Good morning."

"Yes."

"It's good to see you awake," she said.

"I don't remember anything."

"You don't remember making love to me?"

"No."

She put disappointment on her face, then smiled and ran an index finger around his stomach.

"Relax, you were unconscious," she said. "Nothing happened."

"It didn't?"

"No," she said. "We put it off until now."

She swung on top, her stomach to his, her chest to his, her legs spread, her breath hot on his face.

"Time to pay up," she said.

"For what?"

"For all the stitches."

"You did those?"

She nodded.

"Every one of them. I gave you a shot too, for infection. Now it's time for you to show me how grateful you are." She straddled his chest and then inched up until she was on his face. "Love it," she said. "Love it like you stole it."

He complied.

After a shower, Teffinger wandered downstairs to find Johnnie Rail outside by the pool with Evil Angel, drinking coffee and eating from a tray of pastries. The man had a classic front-man look, a modern-day Jim Morrison, with thick shoulder-length black hair, eyes that had seen the world from a path less traveled, and a lean but agile body that didn't seem to have been beaten to death with bad habits.

"Baby," Rail said. "That was her name."

Teffinger sat down.

"Whose name?"

"The land cruiser," he said. "She was the first vehicle I ever owned. Bought her for five hundred pounds back when I was seventeen, working the kitchens by day and trying to get a band going by night. Everyone thought I was crazy. They were partly right, I mean, who needs a four-wheel drive in London, especially one with the steering wheel on the wrong side? But she had some swag and was big enough to carry gear. I'll be honest, my instinct last night was to kill you for killing her, but I didn't."

"Apparently not," Teffinger said. "I'll make it right. I'll get her fixed, if that's possible, or replace her; whatever you want."

"Don't worry about it," Rail said. "I've got the money and at this point we're sort of related, anyway."

Teffinger wrinkled his face.

"How's that?"

"Evil Angel," he said. "We've both engaged her finer side."

Evil Angel smiled.

Teffinger shrugged.

"Do you have any extra coffee?"

"Absolutely. Then you can tell me why you tried to kill me last night."

"I didn't try to kill you," Teffinger said. "I was only trying to get your attention."

Rail clinked his cup against Teffinger's.

"Well, mission accomplished."

Teffinger's phone rang; it was Sydney. "The dead woman down by Tarzan's place is someone named Nicole Carter. She's an attorney in San Francisco in a mega-firm called Taylor, Robinson & Lee."

"Hold on."

He got up and headed for privacy on the other side of the pool, saying to Rail, "Excuse me a minute, I need to take this."

"No problem."

To Sydney, "What was she doing in Denver?"

"According to a guy named Michael Ross, who's the head of the division where she works, which is the litigation division, she was on vacation. She wasn't here on work. Here's the big news, though. We found the note."

"Where? What'd it say?"

"There was an old pop can about twenty feet from her body," she said. "It was in there. It said, KK."

"KK?"

"Right," she said. "I'm assuming it stands for Kovi-Ke. What I'm not sure about is whether it means she's next or whether it was her signature, taking responsibility for the murder. I've tried to call her about twenty times. She's not answering. Her phone's completely off so I can't even track her. I have no idea where she is."

32

June 8
Sunday Morning

The villa was awash in the aftermath of last night's revelries. Glasses and trash were everywhere. Dozens of beer bottles laid in drunken death at the bottom of the pool. A cushion floated on the surface. Teffinger picked up a book of matches and set one on fire as he headed back over to Rail and Evil Angel. They watched him as he came, curious, but in different ways and for different reasons.

Teffinger sat down, looked Rail in the eyes and said, "Here's the problem. I have a friend named Modeste. Someone took her."

Rail washed his face in confusion.

"Me?"

Teffinger shrugged.

"I don't know. You tell me."

Rail shook his head in denial.

"I don't know anyone by that name," he said. "And I don't take people. I make music. I don't know why you're barking up my tree but it's the wrong one."

"She took your little gold bars and your little diamond divas. You figured it out."

Rail's face tightened.

"Who is she?"

Teffinger frowned.

"I'm not here to play word games," he said. "I want her back and I want her now."

"I don't have her," Rail said. "You think that because I have a motive that I'm the one who took her? Do you have any idea how many people have that same motive? The word's out, my man; it's out far and wide; everything's out there for the grabbing. It's not just me looking for it. It's everyone. Hell, I've heard rumors that people have come in from as far as New York looking for it." He paused and added, "If you really want her back, tell me what you know."

Teffinger looked for lies and found none.

"Widson Danticat," he said. "He came for her. Unfortunately, I was with her at the time and it didn't work out for him. He ended up with a broken bottle in his face."

Rail grunted with disgust.

"Danticat's a nobody who does dirty work for whoever has the money," Rail said. "One of his primary clients is a voodoo woman named Janjak." He retreated in thought and added, "It would make sense that she figured out about your friend. She has ways to see things that can't be seen."

Teffinger nodded.

"I found a voodoo tape in Danticat's apartment. The connection is definitely there. Where can I find her?"

Rail shook his head.

"You don't find her," he said. "She finds you."

"Not this time. Give me an address."

Rail frowned.

"You can't do this alone," he said. "I'll help but here's the deal. You get your friend back, assuming she's still alive. I get my stuff back, though; all of it. She keeps none of it. You keep none of it."

"I don't want it," Teffinger said. "If we get her back, you need to leave her alone afterwards. I don't want you tracking her down for revenge. Everyone walks away."

"Deal."

Rail held his hand out.

Teffinger shook it.

"She never really planned to take anything in the first place," Teffinger said. "It sort of fell into her hands."

He told Rail the story—how Modeste came to the villa to take the job offered by May-May, how she found everyone dead, how the bags were right there for the taking, how she picked Teffinger up on the plane for protection, which is how he knew about everything.

What he didn't tell the man is how Modeste sold the gold in New York and wedged the money into a Cayman account. Nor did he tell him that he had the diamond divas buried under the sand down the road, or how Modeste's friend, Constance, still had one of them—Marilyn.

Rail listened to every word, stood up and said, "Give me ten minutes. Then we have work to do." He grabbed Evil Angel's hand. "You come with me."

33

June 8
Sunday Morning

Alone, Teffinger poured another cup of coffee and took the opportunity to call Station Smith. "You still alive?"

"Alive and well," she said.

"You're laying low, I hope."

"Pretty much."

"No, not pretty much," he said. "Do it fully. Things haven't quieted down yet. In fact they might be worse than ever." He took a sip. "I have a weird question for you. I'm in Haiti and I came across a videotape of a voodoo ceremony. There was a woman there who looked a lot like you. Was it, by any chance?"

Silence.

"Station, are you there?"

"I'm here."

Her voice sounded like a spider was crawling up her leg.

"It was you," Teffinger said.

"Nick, stay out of it," she said. "Get the hell out of Haiti. You'll end up dead and so will other people. Don't call me anymore."

The line died.

Teffinger dialed back but the woman didn't pick up.

He called Sydney and said, "Any signs yet of Kovi-Ke?"

"No, none."

"Do me a favor," he said. "Station was involved in some kind of voodoo ritual down here in Haiti, I'm not sure exactly when but I'm guessing not too long ago. Go talk to her and get the details. Don't let her push you off. Get answers. I want to know who did it to her—I suspect it's a voodoo woman down here they call Janjak but I want to know for sure. Find out when it happened and how it came about; and most importantly, why didn't she tell me about it? "

"Nick, it's Sunday—"

"Yeah, I know."

"I've got plans to go see Vivid Black."

He knew the band. He'd caught them at the Taste of Colorado last year and they were awesome.

"You'll have to see them another time," he said. "Be sure Station still has her bodyguards. Oh, one more thing. Ask her if she's ever been able to see through someone else's eyes."

"You're kidding, right?"

"I wish I was. Oh, one more thing."

"That's two things."

He smiled.

"Station told me to get out of Haiti or I'd end up dead and so would other people. Find out who she was talking about. Who else will die?"

He was about to hang up when Sydney said, "Nick, are you still there?"

"Yes."

"I don't think I got a chance to tell you yet," she said. "Remember when you asked me to talk to Kovi-Ke about the other two murders she saw?"

"Yes."

"Well, I did that," she said. "Do you have time to hear about them?"

"Absolutely."

"One of was Faren White, a San Francisco woman, killed three years ago. The other was Jaylor Colt, killed four years ago. Get this, she was a Cuban diplomat who got killed in Washington, D.C."

"How'd you get their names?"

"Leigh Sandt."

"She's helping?"

"God, Nick, she doesn't blame you for what happened to Poppy. I've talked to both of the detectives in charge. Neither remembers any notes being found at the scene but they're going to send me their whole files. I'll forward them to you as soon as I get them. I'm hoping that's tomorrow."

"Find out if either of them have been to Haiti," he said.

"Oh, on a different note, something weird happened with that dead lawyer down by Tarzan's place," Sydney said.

"How weird?"

"Weird enough. She makes big bucks but she was staying at a fleabag down on Colfax. She wasn't using her real name, either. She was using the name Melody Pincher."

"How'd you find out?"

"When she got to Denver she rented a car under her real name," Sydney said. "It had a GPS that showed the vehicle at the hotel during the nights, from about midnight until six in the morning. The manager recognized her as Melody

Pincher. Unfortunately, if someone came to see her we don't know about it. The hotel had only one security camera and it wasn't working. Her room, 201, opened onto an exterior landing that fed down to the parking lot."

She filled him with details for another five minutes. He hadn't hung up for more than ten seconds when Rail appeared.

"Let's go," the man said.

Teffinger stood up, downed what was left of his coffee, and fell into step.

34

June 8
Sunday Morning

Teffinger expected Rail to take him to some kind of a voodoo haunt in the guts of the city, with skulls and jars stuffed with submersed organs and things he didn't understand and didn't want to understand. Instead, they ended up twenty miles south, on a beaten single-lane road that went on forever before it finally dead-ended at the ocean.

Rail stopped a quarter-mile short, turned the vehicle around so it was in escape mode, and killed the engine.

"Her place is up there around the bend," he said.

Teffinger grabbed the man's wrist.

"Wait here."

"Why?"

"Because we're both better off if I do this alone." Rail wrinkled his face, not liking the idea. "Don't worry, I'm not trying to cut you out," Teffinger added. "Wait here."

Then he was gone.

Around the bend aqua water came into view, lapping softly

at a silky sand beach. A jeep and several other vehicles were stationary near a couple of thatched structures that looked like garages or outposts. A barefoot man sitting on the ground in the shade had his back against a wall. His head was bent forward and a hat dipped over his face, in siesta mode. His shirt was off and his chest was ripped with muscles. Next to him, leaning against the structure, was a rifle.

Other than him, there was no sign of life.

A rowboat was pulled up on the sand, just out of the water's grip.

Three or four hundred yards offshore a small island made of sand and palms rose out of the water, the whole thing not being much larger than a football field. The thatched roofs of three or four structures were visible on the far side. On the beach were a handful of rowboats.

Modeste was there.

She was being held captive in one of the structures.

Teffinger could feel her.

His eyes fell back to the rowboat. It wasn't more than thirty steps from mister rifle. If the guy woke up, Teffinger would be an easy target, not only on the beach but also all the way on the row over. One shot, even if it missed him, would alert whoever was on the island.

He'd be a mouse between two snakes.

He retreated into the palms, stripped down to his boxers, hid his clothes in the foliage and made his way on quick but quiet feet to the water's edge. Then he was in with only his head showing, paddling with his hands and legs under the surface in a sidestroke as he made his way slowly towards the island. From the shore, it hadn't looked that far. He now realized it was a dangerous distance, maybe farther than his mediocre-at-best skills would allow, particularly given the recent stitches to his body.

The water, cool at first, now felt like a bath.

He paced himself, intent on not running out of breath or exerting himself so hard that he pulled the stitches out.

It took an insufferable time but he finally got close enough to where his feet mercifully touched bottom. He caught his breath, saw no one, and started towards the water's edge in chest deep water.

Something brushed his leg.

It was a shark, undeniably, a small one, maybe only four feet or so, but definitely enough to rip him to shreds if it got the notion into its prehistoric brain.

He didn't let himself panic.

Instead he stood still until the sinister shadow moved away. Then he pushed his way to the water's edge and scurried across the beach into the palms, where he fell to the sand, rolled onto his back and let one thought and one thought only play in his mind, namely that he made it; he was there; he didn't drown or get eaten in the process.

Getting back would be different.

Strength-wise, he doubted he could do that twice in one day, not without a good long rest. Emotion-wise, he wasn't sure he could get back into shark-infested waters, however uneventful the encounter with the baby had been, especially since now, on examination, a stitch had pulled out and the wound had opened enough to let blood drip.

He closed his eyes.

The darkness felt like whiskey.

He let his body rest and his lungs fill with air.

Suddenly something tapped his chest.

It was the barrel of a rifle in the hands of a large man with a serious face, one that was ready for fighting if Teffinger was stupid enough to take things there. Three equals were beside him; armed men with mean attitudes.

"Up," the man said.

35

June 8
Sunday Afternoon

They led him across the island, winding through the palms and brush, to the opposite side where there was a large structure surrounded by several thatched outbuildings. They made their way past the structures to the beach. Out in the water forty or fifty yards distant was yet another small island, a circular satellite of sand not much more than fifty feet across, holding a few trees and breaking the water's surface by only a marginal amount. The sand between here and there was submersed under the water only a few feet.

The rifle pushed into Teffinger's back.

"Move!"

He turned, saw poison in the man's eyes, and stepped into the water, which was incredibly warm and rose only to his waist as he headed across.

At the island he found something he didn't expect.

On the far side, lying face down on a blanket near the water's edge, was a woman; a woman with very dark skin, wearing a white bikini bottom and no top. She turned her face briefly towards Teffinger as he approached, too fast for him to make out her features. When he got to her she said, "Rub my back."

Her voice was deep.

Her back wasn't normal.

It was covered with scars, a hundred or more, each about two inches long, as if they had been individually carved in with the tip of a blade, not stitched, and allowed to close on their own, resulting in wounds that were slightly raised and visibly lighter than her skin tone.

"Are you Janjak?"

The woman didn't raise her head or show her face, which was hidden against her arm and under long, black dreadlocks.

"Yes," she said. "Rub my back."

Teffinger knelt down in the sand and complied.

The woman's muscles were taut.

Her body was strong and shapely, an equal to Kovi-Ke's.

Her skin glistened with heat.

"I'm looking for a friend," he said. "Her name is Modeste."

"I know why you're here, Mr. Teffinger," she said. "We'll get to all that in due time. Right now, the only thing you need to worry about is my back."

Teffinger had questions but kept his mouth shut.

He worked at the woman's back for a good five minutes. Then she spread her feet apart ever so slightly and said, "Do my ass and my legs."

"Where's Modeste?"

"We'll get to that," she said. "Just keep rubbing."

Teffinger complied, working from her lower back down to her feet and then up again.

He still hadn't seen her face.

As more and more time passed, the more he pictured it as burnt or disfigured, and he prepared himself to keep any repulsion off his expression when she eventually displayed it.

Finally, she turned over.

Her face wasn't disfigured but it wasn't pretty, either; not to imply it was ugly, it wasn't; it was somewhere there in the middle. Her lips were large and her teeth had a slight, almost imperceptible, touch of gray in them. Her breasts, on full uninhibited display, were small, almost boyish, but her chest and arms and stomach were strong and in their prime. She looked to be about thirty.

"You killed one of my men," she said. "You threw a bottle into his face. That wasn't very nice."

"So, he was working for you, then."

"Yes."

"And the other men too? The ones who took Modeste?"

"No, they weren't mine."

"Then whose were they?"

"Johnnie Rail's."

Teffinger shook his head.

"I don't think so."

"Think what you want," she said. "I'll make you a deal. You do something for me and in return I'll let you search anywhere you want. Satisfy yourself." Around her neck was a razorblade on a chain. She took it off, handed it to Teffinger and said, "Cut a two-inch notch in my back. Don't cross any of the ones that are already there. Be sure it's deep enough to leave a scar." She lay down on her stomach, exposing her back.

Teffinger pictured sinking the edge of the blade into her flesh.

"No."

"You can't search unless you do it," she said. "Do you want to search or not?"

He did.

So he did it.

Afterwards she licked the blood off the razorblade, hung it around her neck and shouted to one of the men, "Let him search everywhere he wants. He has complete freedom for as long as he wants. When he's done, let him leave. No one is to harm him." Then to Teffinger, "Nice to meet you, Mr. Teffinger. Be careful of Johnnie Rail."

He stood up.

His hand shook.

"Let me ask you something," he said. "Did you do a voodoo ritual on a Jamaican woman named Kovi-Ke?"

"Yes."

"How about a Denver woman named Station Smith?"

"Yes. She's dead, by the way."

"Not quite," he said. "I talked to her just this morning."

"Whatever you say. Go now. This session is done. I'll see you at the next one."

Teffinger didn't know what the words meant and didn't want to.

He left.

36

June 8
Sunday Afternoon

Escorted by an armed man, Teffinger was given khaki pants, a white cotton shirt and leather sandals, followed by free reign to search the island for Modeste. She wasn't there, he knew that deep down, otherwise he wouldn't be allowed to look. Could Janjak be telling the truth that it was Rail's men who took her? Did Rail script Janjak in as the bad guy, possibly in hopes that she'd kill Teffinger?

Teffinger searched the largest structure—Janjak's quarters—first, not limiting himself to the obvious, but also testing for trap doors and hidden compartments, coming up with nothing time and time again.

Next was the closest outbuilding; a flimsy wooden structure with a thatched roof; not built to weather any type of serious storm; probably used for storage of some sort.

It had no windows.

The only entry, a wooden door, was padlocked.

The man didn't have the key and didn't know who did.

"Shoot it off," Teffinger said.

The man hesitated, shook his head and said, "We'll come back."

Teffinger kicked the door, again and again and again, until it busted opened.

Inside it was dark.

The floor was dirt.

Teffinger stepped in to spot something in the corner, at first glance appearing to be a body lying on a blanket, and then definitely so.

He headed over and kneeled down.

To his utter shock it was Modeste.

Her lower lip was cut and swollen.

Her eye was bruised purple.

He shook her.

She didn't respond but she wasn't dead.

She was breathing.

She had a pulse.

Around her ankle was a leg iron, padlocked to a chain that disappeared under the wall to somewhere outside, no doubt secured to something solid.

Teffinger stood up.

He needed to get the woman out of there.

He needed to take down the man with the rifle.

Suddenly a figure appeared in the doorway, a black silhouette against the light. It was Janjak. By the time Teffinger realized she was raising a blow dart to her lips, it was too late. She blew and with an eerie swish a dart rocketed through the air and stabbed into Teffinger's chest.

He jerked it out.

"You should have never come here," Janjak said.

Suddenly everything in Teffinger's brain shifted.

Something was in his blood, something evil, something intent on taking him down. He fought against it but it did no good. His knees buckled and he dropped to the dirt. Then everything turned black.

37

June 8
Sunday Evening

Teffinger regained consciousness to find himself adrift in a rowboat, surrounded by nothing but water, with no land in sight. His right wrist was handcuffed to a motor mount at the stern of the vessel. At the bow of the vessel was a makeshift wooden mast, bolted into the wood, rising six or seven feet at a diagonal into the air. At the top of that post was a human skull.

It was early twilight, meaning he'd been unconscious for some time.

There was no telling how far he was out to sea. It might be two miles, if might be fifty. He had no idea if he was in a shipping lane or in one of those no-man's-lands that humans hadn't seen in the last hundred years.

His skin, where exposed during the day, was raw and dry.

There were no oars.

There was no food and, worse, no water. The realization made the sandpaper sensation in his throat even drier. His instinct was to quench his needs with the seawater, but he remembered the old sailor stories of how it was the devil's drink that would spiral a weak soul into insanity and death.

He resisted, at least for now.

He scouted the horizon in all directions.

Nothing broke the line, not a mast, not a tree, not a vessel, not a shape of any kind. The only thing left in the universe was an endless expanse of rolling waves, which mercifully, were tranquil enough—at least for the moment—that they didn't breach into the boat.

He turned his attention to the handcuffs.

The end around his wrist was solid.

He couldn't twist out, not in a hundred years.

The other end was around a solid welded piece of the motor mount. The mount itself was affixed to the boat with eight bolts, all rusted tight. They didn't budge.

Kicking the boards out wasn't an option.

The back of the boat would be off at that point.

The boat would sink and Teffinger would still be affixed to the motor mount, which had to be a good thirty pounds; it would be his own little personal anchor down into a watery grave.

He was stuck.

He tried to relax and not let himself panic. Someone would come along; a fisherman, or some couple on their retirement yacht navigating the world; or maybe a pontoon plane, island hopping for remote sand and beach drinks. Someone had to. He'd done too many good things in his life for the world to let him die like this. If there were any sense of real karma in the world, he wouldn't be abandoned in his time of need.

The thought felt good but wilted all too soon.

Bad things happened to good people all the time. In fact, that was his job—straightening those kinds of things out;

and why? Because the world didn't do it on its own, that's why. Because there was no karma, there was only clean up. And speaking of good people, if the truth be told, how good was he, really, when you looked way deep down?

He broke hearts.

He had more than his share of selfish moments.

The minutes passed.

The sun sank lower and lower.

Night was coming.

The wind picked up.

A slight chop marked the surface of the water.

Then long rollers came in, the kind that had been on the march for many tens of miles, maybe even hundreds, gently rising the boat in a long steady motion to a crest and then just as slowly dropping it down into a valley.

They weren't dangerous; at least not yet.

The night could be long.

It could be his last.

Anything could happen.

He needed to prepare himself for it.

He needed to reach down and gather every ounce of strength he had.

It was almost dark when something unexpected happened. A vessel suddenly appeared from out of nowhere in the distance not more than a kilometer off, cresting a roller at the same time as Teffinger.

His blood raced.

He stood up as much as he could and waved his free arm back and forth with a desperate energy.

"Hey! Over here! Come on, see me! Come on, look this

way! Look this way!"

It must have spotted him because it seemed to change course and head his way.

Yes!

It had seen him!

It was definitely heading right for him!

As it approached, it took the shape of a small fishing vessel, not more than twenty-five or thirty feet long, with an outrigger on each side.

It stopped fifty feet short.

"Help me!" Teffinger shouted. "I'm stuck on this boat. I'm going to die."

Two fishermen were at the bow, dressed in torn clothes.

Instead of shouting back, they locked in argument. A third man, the one who had been driving, joined them. The words became animated. The discussion seemed to be about the skull, the human skull floating out there in the middle of nowhere with Teffinger; his buddy, the skull.

After what seemed to be a long time, they retreated from the bow, now apparently of one mind.

Then the boat turned and left.

Teffinger called after it, nonstop, frantic to not be abandoned.

It made no difference.

It kept going until it disappeared out of sight.

He was alone.

Then darkness came.

At first it wasn't full darkness because of the moon. Then clouds rolled in and shut out even the faintest of light. Nothing was left except the painful dryness of his mouth and the rhythmic chop against the side of the boat.

His body begged for sleep.

He fought against it.

He might need to hand-bail. If that became necessary he needed to get on it before the point of no return got him in a death grip. It wouldn't take much more wind for the water to chop up to where it would breach the boat. He needed to be awake if that happened.

Live 'till dawn.

Just get that far and then take it from there.

DAY SIX

June 9
Monday

38

June 9
Monday Morning

The night was filled with demons. Teffinger spent most of it scooping invisible waves out of the bottom of the boat with his one free hand in a desperate struggle to keep the freeboard above the water's surface, never able to see through the blackness of the night to access exactly how precarious things were, or weren't, but ever fearing the capsize would come within the next few seconds unless he ignored his burning muscles and kept in motion.

He went on and on and on, until he could go on no more; until death was no longer the worst of the options; until his body shut down and gave up and damn the consequences.

Sleep took him; no, not sleep, something much more extreme than sleep, something more like a descent into a black vortex where there was no sound or sight or smell or feeling or emotion or thoughts.

It gripped him with gorilla strength and squeezed every ounce of conscious life out of him.

He saw it coming.

He knew its strength.

It was so powerful that he could drown without even knowing it.

He didn't care.

Everyone had to die at some point.

This was as good a time as any.

A pressure on his wrist worked its way into his consciousness. He focused, expecting it to disappear, but it stayed and if anything became even more pronounced. He let himself slip to a higher level of awareness, knowing he was leaving the sanctuary of where he was but needing to know what was happening.

He opened his eyes.

Someone was sawing at the handcuff with a hacksaw.

"Stay still."

The words came from a familiar voice.

They belonged to Johnnie Rail.

The man's face came into focus. Behind it, the sky was bright. It was well into the day. Rail held a canteen to Teffinger's mouth and said, "Drink."

He obliged.

It saturated his mouth and lips and throat and, as it did, his brain ignited with the realization that he would live.

He would live.

He would live.

He would live.

39

June 9
Monday Morning

Rail and his first mate, Evil Angel, got Teffinger out of the rowboat and into a twenty-six foot Boston Whaler with double Johnson outboards, at which point Rail pulled a pistol, pointed it at the rowboat and said, "Bye bye, baby."

"Wait," Teffinger said.

"Why?"

"Get the skull first."

"No, it's cursed."

"It's evidence," Teffinger said.

"Evidence of what?"

"I'm not sure but maybe someone named Poppy."

Rail shook his head.

"I'm not messing with that thing, not now, not in a hundred years."

Then he shot six rounds into the floorboard. Water slowly filtered up through the holes, taking some time before filling the boat, which then sank at the stern with the weight of the motor mount. The bow pointed upward, breaking the surface but not by much, a foot at best.

Teffinger's chest pounded.

The boat, as it now floated, wouldn't be buoyant enough to support his weight, not to mention the handcuff to the stern would have pulled his head underwater. He would have died if the boat had capsized, plain and simple.

The skull hung a couple of feet diagonal above the surface. Rail put two rounds into it, enough to send it to Davy Jones' Locker for eternity.

"Let's go," he said. "We're fifty miles out."

Rail's appearance wasn't an accident. Hidden on the shore yesterday, he'd spotted Janjak's men towing the rowboat out to sea. The skull was a warning to anyone who might offer assistance; especially fishermen, it was a curse to their catch and to their souls, not just today but forever. When Rail got back to the vehicle it was gone, confiscated by Janjak's men no doubt. He hiked out, hour after hour after hour, finally getting to a crossroad where he was able to hitch a ride into Port-au-Prince. He called Evil Angel, who brought money and food. They rented a Boston Whaler and set out to sea at full throttle as twilight settled in.

The chances of finding Teffinger were remote at best.

Out there, Rail realized just how impossible it was, especially in the dark.

They spent the night at the villa.

In the morning, the marine radios buzzed with fishermen warning each other about a cursed man in a rowboat over near graveyard's point. Rail and Evil Angel headed for it, searched for hours and eventually got lucky.

Now, at this moment, the ocean danced with long rolling

swells but the surface was relatively free of chop, making for a smooth and even enjoyable ride.

Teffinger was alive.

He had water in his body.

Soon he'd have food.

He told Rail everything that happened after they separated yesterday, namely meeting Janjak on the beach, her attempt to make Teffinger believe that Rail had Modeste, carving her back, searching at her request and finding Modeste, unconscious and roughed up but alive.

"I don't get the back thing," he said.

Rail frowned.

"That's one of the way she gets souls," he said. "She was trying to steal yours. If you died before the wound sealed and scared over, your soul would have entered her. When the wound seals, your soul's locked in. It can't get back out until and unless the wound is reopened. That's why she told you not to carve over any of the existing scars."

Teffinger exhaled.

"Do you actually believe that?"

"It doesn't matter what I believe. She believes it. Those fishermen who left you to die, they believe it." He smiled and added, "You look like death by the way."

Teffinger exhaled.

"You should see it from my angle. Time's running out on Modeste. What about the local police? Can we tap them?"

Rail smirked, negative.

"The first thing they'll do is figure out you threw a bottle into a man's face. They'll have a foreigner in jail, which means money, which is a very, very good thing, and gets better the longer they leave you in. The second thing they'll do is stay the hell away from Janjak. Why? Because they're not crazy."

As the vessel crested a roller, over the bow far in the distance a sliver a land appeared at the horizon.

"Land," Teffinger said. "So it's up to us."

"It always has been."

Evil Angel spotted a first aid kit latched under the console near Rail's feet. Inside was burn lotion, which she gently applied to Teffinger's face with her tender little Hong Kong fingers. It went on like an icy oasis.

"Us finding you was fate," she said. "Fate can't be denied."

40

June 9
Monday Afternoon

Securely and safely on land at Rail's villa, Teffinger put enough food in his gut to get his strength back and then set off alone down the beach to mull options to get Modeste back, none of which were coming up particularly pretty.

Ten minutes into it, Evil Angel came charging from behind, knocked him to the sand and pinned him down. She moved her body up until she straddled his chest. "Don't blow it."

"Blow what?"

"Your life," she said. "You've been given a second chance. Stay away from Janjak."

"I wish it was that easy."

She wiggled on him.

"Rail believes in her powers," she said.

"What about you?"

"She scares me like nothing else, I know that much."

Teffinger moved to get up but Evil Angel sunk all her weight on him. He flipped her over and pinned her down, holding her arms up over her head.

"Now who's on the bottom?"

She lifted her head to kiss him.

He pulled back. Then just as fast something snapped in his brain, something primitive and primeval. He lowered his head and let his lips meet hers.

"What's the deal with you and Rail?"

"I help manage the band," she said. "He screws me when he's not busy doing something else. That's it."

"Are you two a thing?"

"You mean romantically?"

"Yes."

She smiled.

"No. What we have, if you could even call it having something, is purely physical. He doesn't care what you do to me, if that's what you're worrying about. No one's going to get on your case or get mad at you."

Teffinger's chest pounded.

He got to his feet, picked the woman up and carried her to the water's edge, where he lowered into the wet sand. There he pulled off her clothes and took her as the warm salty water lapped up and around their bodies and the sun played on his back.

Nothing had ever felt so good.

Nothing ever would.

Afterwards they left their clothes on the sand and walked down the beach hand in hand, naked, without a soul around, with only the sun and the surf and the horizon line. Kovi-Ke played in Teffinger's mind but only as a faint shadow. It was strange to think that just a few days ago he was infatuated with her, even knowing she was a killer or somehow mixed up with one—he still hadn't figured that one out. In fact, he was in Haiti right now because of her. She was the reason he met Evil Angel.

Maybe there was such a thing as fate.

"I'm just going to call you Angel from now on," he said. "No Evil."

She smiled.

Then she grew serious.

"Nick, I want to tell you something but you have to promise to keep it to yourself."

Her face was tense.

"What's going on?"

"You know the stuff that Rail's trying to get back? The gold and the diamonds?"

"Yes."

"Well, there's a reason," she said. "He stole the diamonds. They're not his."

"I thought the guy was a rock star."

"He is."

"So why would he do something that stupid? Wasn't life already good enough for him?"

"It's a long story," Angel said. "The bottom line is he sort of stumbled into a situation where the whole thing got too easy to not just do. He had a foolproof plan where no one would ever figure out it was him. In hindsight, he was stupid."

"Who'd he steal them from?"

"A Hong Kong man by the name of Kong."

"That's where you're from."

She nodded.

"What I told you before about helping to manage the band is true," she said. "What I didn't tell you is that I have another duty, which is to keep my eyes and ears on Kong to know when and if he ever figures out that Rail was the one behind the theft. When that happens, Rail will have to run and run fast. His rock star days will be over."

"How to you keep your eyes and ears on Kong?"

"I have my ways," she said. "I'm telling you this because I could fail at my job without knowing it. Kong could come marching down the beach right now, with everything figured out and without my knowing it. I'm hoping that doesn't happen but it's a possibility that both Rail and me have to live with. And you."

"Meaning what?"

"Meaning anyone close to Rail at this point in his life is in danger," she said. "Kong might think you're implicated. He'd peel your skin off with a potato knife just to find out if he was right or not. Those diamonds are no ordinary stones. They're world-class. They're some of the largest ever found. They're worth tens of millions. My advice to you is to get away from Rail."

An image flashed in Teffinger's brain, an image from this morning, of Rail suddenly appearing at the rowboat and sawing the handcuff off Teffinger's wrist.

"He saved my life."

"Technically that's true," Angel said. "But he didn't do it because that's his basic nature. He did it to save himself. You're the best link he has to the diamonds."

Teffinger chewed on it.

It tasted sour but it also tasted real.

"What's he going to do if he gets the diamonds back? Return them?"

"Yes."

"What about the gold?"

"The gold was his," she said. "It was a loss but not a matter of life or death. He's not destitute even without it. The diamonds, that's the big thing."

Teffinger silently focused on the fact that he had the diamonds buried in the sand down the road, all but Marilyn, which he could secure easily enough.

He could give them to Rail right now.

He could save Rail's life, right now.

Ten minutes ago he would have done that, for the sole reason that Rail had saved his life. But now, knowing the real reason Rail did what he did, well, Teffinger was less indebted.

He needed to weigh giving the diamonds back to Rail so the man could live versus keeping them as a bargaining chip to possibly trade for Modeste.

Whose life was worth more?

No, that wasn't the question.

The question was, whose life was in the most danger right at this exact moment in time?

Modeste.

Rail's danger was in the future and, in fact, might never materialize.

The answer became clear.

He needed to keep the diamonds hidden.

He needed to concentrate on Modeste.

He looked at Angel.

"Tell me something," he said. "Why would you risk the wrath of Kong? Rail can't be paying you enough."

"I owe him."

"In what way? Why?"

"He did something for me once upon a time," she said. "Something big. Let's just leave it at that."

"Does Kong know that you owe Rail?"

"No. At least I don't think so."

41

41

June 9
Monday Afternoon

Teffinger borrowed Angel's cell phone, dialed his own and got no answer, which was good because it meant it was probably still on the beach with his clothes at Janjak's and hadn't been stumbled on yet. Then he dialed Sydney in Denver.

She answered with all the subtleness of a storm.

"Nick, I've called you twenty times."

"Did anyone answer?"

"No."

"Good. I lost that phone. Kill it for me."

"You need to get back here," she said. "Did you hear about Station?"

His chest pounded.

"No. Hear what?"

"She was murdered."

"That can't be," he said. "I talked to her just yesterday morning."

"It happened yesterday afternoon."

"How?"

"Someone slit her throat. Her body was found in a boxcar at that industrial rail yard on the north edge of town, the one off Quebec. Her car was parked at the edge of the yard."

"How about a note? Did you find one?"

"Yes," she said. "It was a ways off this time, fifty yards at least. We found it in an envelope that was duct taped to a light post. The envelope was completely covered. You didn't even know it was there until you unwrapped all the tape. It could have stayed there for years."

"What'd it say?"

"Red sky at morning."

"Red sky at morning?"

"Yes."

"It might have something to do with that old rhyme," Sydney said. "You know the one I'm talking about?"

"No."

"Red sky at morning, sailors take warning. Red sky at night, sailor's delight."

"How about Kovi-Ke?"

"Still AWOL."

Teffinger exhaled, trying to not reach the conclusion he was getting forced into. The resistance did no good.

"Put a warrant out for her."

"Are you serious?"

"Unfortunately, I am."

"Nick, the chief wants you back here, as in the day before yesterday."

"Tell him I'll be there as soon as I can."

"Which is when?"

"I don't know. I'll call you tomorrow."

"Nick, you're going to end up fired—"

He punched off.

His gut churned.

He'd failed.

He'd made bad decisions.

Station was dead because of him.

He'd been warned that she was going to be murdered and did he stay in Denver and tend to business? Did he do one simple thing to protect her other than tell her to get a bodyguard? Did he dig down to where the answers were, the ones that might have saved her?

No.

No.

No.

No and no again.

Nick, you're going to end up fired.

At this point, that would probably be in everyone's best interest. If someone capable was in his job, Station might still be alive right now.

Maybe it was time to step aside.

Maybe he should just quit; do it right now, this minute; just call the chief and get it over with before he chickened out.

He headed outside and down the beach, deciding.

One thing for sure, he wasn't going to step back from Modeste. He wasn't going to make the same mistake he did with Station. He'd either get her back or die trying.

Screw everything else.

42

June 9
Monday Afternoon

Rail had company when Teffinger got back to the villa, a good-looking man in his late forties, white, clean-shaved, with a full head of black hair combed straight back, a man who moved with confidence and looked like he'd be equally at home in a board room or on a sailboat, dressed in khakis and a blue button-down shirt.

"Teffinger, meet Stephen Blake, my IP attorney out of New York."

They shook hands.

The man had a solid grip.

"New York, huh?"

"Coran, Night & Cage," Blake said. "Maybe you've heard of us?"

"Sorry, no. I've heard of New York, though."

The man smiled.

Rail said, "Copyright, that's the name of the game. Everything I do, and I mean everything, whether it's writing a line of lyrics, a guitar riff, a whole song, everything, Stephen gets it copyrighted for me, worldwide, before anyone else in the world knows it exists, outside the band of course. It's an upfront cost but it saves a ton of litigation down the line when someone comes out of the blue and tries to say you stole it from them."

"Sounds logical," Teffinger said.

Blake nodded.

"It's the only way to go. The world's filled with thieves and lowlifes. Unfortunately, Johnnie and everyone like him are walking targets."

"I'd imagine so."

Rail said, "He also does copyright enforcement, cease and desist letters, that kind of thing, although to be honest I don't really give a rat's ass if someone else steals my stuff. My primary concern is that no one claims that I stole theirs. I have a reputation to uphold." Teffinger must have had a look on his face because Rail added, "Give us an hour or so to finish up. Then I'm all yours."

Teffinger shook Blake's hand.

"Heading back today?"

"Morning, actually."

With a wink at Teffinger, Rail slapped the lawyer on the back and said, "There are some pretty good women down in Port-au-Prince. Not that much money, either."

Stephen shrugged.

"A man's got to have his vices."

An hour later Sydney called.

"I just talked to Station's sister, Melinda," she said. "She had quite the story."

"In what way?"

"Two years ago there were four of them on a 38-foot sailboat, Station and Melinda and their two boyfriends at the time, guys named John Vesten, who was with Station, and Danny-Dan Jones, who was with Melinda. They charted the vessel in Jamaica and were sailing to the Dominican Republic on a two-week trip. When they passed by Haiti, they were boarded and Station was taken. The other three were held at gunpoint until the next day, at which point Station was returned. That night, she was subjected to some kind of voodoo ritual."

"Did anyone report it?"

"No, they were under threat of murder if anyone ever said anything to anybody," Sydney said. "They made a pact and kept it secret all this time."

"Janjak," Teffinger said.

"So you think she killed Station?"

"That's my guess, through Kovi-Ke," he said. "My suspicion is that Kovi-Ke is working for her. What I don't get is why they were playing a game with me. Run down the two guys and see what they know. Tell them they could be targets. Make sure Station's sister knows that too."

"She already does," she said. "I just had a wild thought."

"Like what?"

"Maybe there's been some kind of grand plan in place all along to lure you down to Haiti."

"For what purpose?"

"I don't know. You tell me."

43

June 9
Monday Afternoon

Teffinger came up with a plan; a crazy, dangerous plan; a plan that would probably kill him, but at least it was something. The question at this point is whether he should do it now, this afternoon under light of day, or wait until dark.

Dark make more sense, a lot more sense.

Still, every minute that passed was another strike against Modeste. The clicks of her clock were limited. He paced and then hunted down Angel.

"I need a place where I can keep a prisoner," he said.

"Who?"

"Janjak."

She smiled, anticipating the punch line, and then grew serious when it didn't come.

"You're not kidding."

Teffinger shook his head.

"It can't be here. They'll look for her here."

Ten minutes later they were in the Boston Whaler, cruising

on plane into open turquoise waters. Forty-five minutes later they came to a string of three small islands or cays, none bigger than five or six acres, all within a few hundred yards of one another. They circled around and through, finding hypnotic pristine beaches and swaying palms but not a single sign of human life, not now or from the past, stretching all the way back to the beginning of time

"No one comes here," Angel said. "They're cursed."

"By who?"

"Sea ghosts, if you believe the rumor."

"Well, I don't."

"These used to be rocky crags," she said. "No one ever came here. The ghosts slowly transformed them over time, turning them into paradises. No one could pass by without stopping. The ghosts made bait out of beauty."

"Bait for what?"

She shrugged.

"All anyone knows for sure is that people disappear, boats disappear. There are stories of bad things, supernatural things, things where souls get dragged under the water and are made to live forever with no air."

"So why are you bringing me here?"

"Because you don't believe the stories."

"What about you?"

"I believe lots of boats ran aground here in the dark waters over time and that lots of people unquestionably died," she said. "I believe that rumors can start from events like that."

"That's now an answer."

Teffinger maneuvered the vessel between the three islands, out of sight of open waters, and trimmed the engines up as he drifted into a beach. The bow nestled into the sand.

He tied it off with an anchor, just to be sure, then made his way through the lukewarm water to the dry sand of the beach.

Angel hesitated in the boat.

Then she jumped in the water and joined him.

The beach was pristine and under other circumstances Teffinger could have spent the rest of his life right there with no regrets. The opposite side of the island was no more than a couple of hundred yards over.

They cut across.

Halfway there they came across a human skull lying in the sand. Teffinger picked it up and bounced it in his hand to get a feel for the weight and said, "Here's one of your lost sailors."

"I don't think so. Look."

He did.

Thirty feet away was a pile of bones, a large pile, human skeletons, with twenty or thirty easily identified skulls. None contained flesh.

"Looks like a body dump of some kind," Teffinger said. "Not recently though. These have been here for years, maybe decades."

Angel kept her distance and said, "We should get out of here."

"Are these your ghosts?"

"I don't know."

Teffinger dropped the skull and kept going.

"Let's see what else we have."

What they had for the rest of the island was nature uninterrupted, nature strutting her stuff with all the passion and mystery and eroticism she could command.

"Let's check the other two islands," Teffinger said.

As they passed by the bones on the way back, Angel pointed to something and said, "What's that?"

Teffinger looked.

There was something in the middle of it all, peeking out from under the sand, barely protruding but visible nonetheless, possibly an old belt buckle or the tip of a weapon.

He picked his way through the bones, trying to not step on any but finding them too dense too avoid, feeling the crunch of their once-meaningful fibers shoot up his legs and into his heart.

The object was small and golden.

He wedged it out of the sand.

What it was he couldn't believe.

"A gold coin."

He tossed it to Angel, looked for more in the sand, found nothing and picked his way out.

"It looks Spanish," Angel said.

"Yes it does."

"What do you think it's worth?"

"More than my soul."

"So what's it doing just laying there in the sand?" Angel shifted her footing and ran her eyes over the gluttony of bones. "Maybe there was some kind of pirate fight over bags of gold and that kind of thing. This one got dropped when someone was running."

Teffinger chewed on it.

"Possible," he said.

"It's probably been peeking in and out of the sand for a hundred years. We happened by at the exact right time. I told you there was such a thing as fate. It's our first possession together. We share it, right? Fifty-fifty?"

"It's all yours," Teffinger said. "But if there's more, we'll share them."

"You think there's more?"

He nodded.

"You bury treasure in the sand in a crate or chest of some kind," he said. "It's going to be wooden; possibly reinforced with steel bands and a padlock, but at least to some extent wooden. Time takes its toll. The wood rots and disintegrates. Now the treasure is loose in the sand. Trees grow and roots push things around under the surface. Some of those things get pushed up. Like that little guy, for instance."

"So what are all the bodies for? A marker?"

He nodded.

"A marker and a deterrent," he said. "What's the last place on this island you'd want to poke around in?"

"Right there."

"Exactly."

He rolled his sleeves up and started picking bones out and throwing them to the side. Angel watched for a few heartbeats and then joined in.

"I want to make love to you right there in the middle," she said.

Teffinger smiled.

"You're a kinky little thing."

"You have no idea."

He slapped her ass.

"Maybe that's what all these bodies are," he said. "Maybe they all had the exact same idea. Did you ever think of that?"

She slapped him back.

"You're not getting out of it so don't even try."

44

June 9
Monday Afternoon

The next three hours changed the whole world. As Teffinger predicted—but still to his shock—hundreds of gold coins were buried under the bones, ranging from depths of two to five feet down; 328 precious little golden pieces of history, all told. If they widened the circle they'd probably find a hundred more but that was enough for now. They replaced the sand and the bones, made everything look as undisturbed and original as possible, then collapsed in the shade on their backs as the warm cerulean sky played through the palms.

"Half are yours," Teffinger said. "A hundred sixty nine."

"I don't like to think of it like that," Angel said. "I like to think of it as three twenty eight, ours together."

"I already have a plan for my share."

"What is what?"

"Use them to get Modeste back."

"You're going to give them to Janjak?"

"Some of them," he said. "I'm not sure how many yet."

"That's crazy."

"Why?"

"I don't see why you're going to such extremes," she said. "The woman played you. You owe her nothing."

"I'm all she has."

"Yeah, but you don't owe her anything. Do you hear what I'm saying?"

He got to his feet and pulled Angel up.

They took off their shirts and split the coins, one going into hers then one into his, until they were all divided. Teffinger stuck ten coins in his pocket, tied his shirt off and said, "Stay here."

"Where you going?"

He dangled the shirt.

"To bury this on one of the other islands."

"Why?"

"To keep it safe."

"I'm not coming with you?"

He shook his head.

"It's better you don't know where I'm doing it. That could save your life later."

"You don't trust me?"

"I trust you just fine," he said. "It's other people I don't trust. Stay here."

He made his way to the Boston Whaler, which fired up exactly as it was supposed to, and then motored over to the farther of the other two islands. There he found something he didn't expect—another large grouping of fleshless skeletons, even larger than the first, with a good forty or fifty skulls showing.

He didn't like the looks of it.

He didn't like the island at all.

It had an eerie patina to it, nothing he could put a finger

on but something that didn't resonate well in his gut. He left and went to the other island.

There he found no skeletons.

He found a place to his liking, one he could remember, and buried his shirt three feet deep. The sand went back and then got smoothed out until the dig turned invisible.

Back at the first island, Angel was waiting for him on the beach, meaning she clearly saw where he was coming from. She waded out waist deep into the aqua waters, tossed her shirt in the boat and then climbed in.

He said, "Any ghosts get you?"

She gave him a wet kiss on the lips.

"Only you. You're a ghost, aren't you?"

"You never know."

Two minutes later they were out in open waters on full plane with the wind in their hair and the pounding of the hull in their ears.

Halfway back Teffinger said, "It's best that no one knows anything about any of this for the time being. Put your coins someplace safe but don't tell anyone about them. That includes Rail."

"That's my plan."

"Good. I don't want to find out they're cursed."

45

June 9
Monday Evening

Beaten with exhaustion, Teffinger lapsed into a deep, cavernous sleep when he got back to the villa, not to open his eyes again until hours later when evening was thick over Haiti. He bolted upright with a racing heart, only to find Angel sleeping next to him, already waking from his movement. He didn't remember making love to her or even laying down with her. She must have come in after the fact.

"Can you find those islands in the dark?"

"Maybe."

"Is that a yes or a no?"

"I'd have to go back through the GPS history on my phone to get the coordinates," she said. "Then I'd have to use the phone to try to get back there in the dark."

"Work on it."

The next hour was a fury of motion, but whether it was forward motion or backwards motion, only time would tell. They gassed up the Whaler, stocked it with everything they'd need, and worked on summoning up the courage to actually do what they were thinking of doing. All the while Teffinger twisted his mind trying to decide whether it would be a good thing or a bad one to bring Rail with him. Both scenarios had their pros and cons.

"I'm coming," Rail said. "End of discussion."

"We'll see."

"I've already seen."

In the end, Teffinger relented.

Half an hour after dark, they both kissed Angel goodbye and set off into the black sea with the Whaler's lights out. A pale moon beat through a blanket of high thin clouds, throwing some light to the earth, not much but enough to distinguish the shore from the water.

They made their way down the coast under relatively calm seas until they came to Janjak's lagoon. There they motored quietly to far end of the island, anchored the boat and headed up the sand on foot.

Teffinger had a knife but no gun.

Rail had two weapons, a handgun and a rifle.

Several armed men became visible as Teffinger and Rail studied the grounds from the black recesses of the night. There was no sign of Janjak but the lights of the primary structure were on.

"I count seven," Teffinger said.

"I got eight."

"You ready?"

"No."

Teffinger grunted.

"Stay behind me. The more I think around the rifle, leave it here; it'll just slow us down. Don't shoot anyone unless it's absolutely in self-defense, and then don't shoot to kill. Get them in the leg or something. I don't want to take lives to save one, even if they deserve it. If we get separated, we'll meet at the boat. If I get killed or taken, don't hang around for me. Just get the hell out. Are we on the same page?"

"Yes."

Teffinger exhaled.

"Okay, then. Game time."

With a pounding chest, Teffinger snuck through the night, occasionally turning to make sure Rail was still behind him. He took his time, picking his shadows with all the precision of a surgeon, slowly making his way into the thick of it all and, finally, to the very thatched structure where Modeste had been held prisoner.

The door wasn't locked.

She wasn't there.

That wasn't a surprise.

Teffinger expected it.

They no doubt moved her to a new location, assuming she was still alive. It would be futile to look for her. She could be a hundred different places, none of which were any-where around here.

"Plan B," he whispered to Rail.

"Yeah, I know."

They snuck back out, circled around through the outlying blackness, and from the beach approached the main struc-ture—Janjak's quarters—crawling on their stomachs. The windows were lit from inside, throwing a yellow patina into the night, almost like cat eyes, but no exterior lights were on.

Two men sat at a table of some sorts on the left side of the structure, drinking from bottles. Their weapons leaned near their sides.

Their voices were animated—drunken.

Teffinger and Rail approached from the right, letting the corner mask them.

Then, they were there.

They were right there.

Teffinger worked his way to a window and brought an eye far enough over to look inside.

He saw no one.

They entered, moving quickly, searching for Janjak.

They found her upstairs, in a dark, dark room, sitting in a chair in the corner, staring right at them with the whites of her eyes.

"I've been waiting for you," she said.

"Scream and you're dead," Teffinger said. "All we want is Modeste."

"Me scream? No, don't worry about that. Are you ready to have some fun?"

With lightning speed two men suddenly sprang from out of nowhere. Knuckles landed with the force of a rock to Teffinger's face, exploding the inside of his skull into fireworks and knocking him to the floor.

A kick landed on his ribs, then another, and then another.

He tried to twist away.

It did no good.

The leather hardness of a boot smashed into the side of his head, snapping it so fast that his teeth bit deep into his tongue.

Blood filled his mouth.

He braced for the next blow.

Suddenly a shot rang out, an explosion of gunfire so incredibly thunderous that it felt as if the whole world had just imploded.

It came from Rail.

He pulled Teffinger to his feet and punched Janjak in the face so hard that she collapsed to the floor.

"Get her!" Rail said.

Teffinger flung the woman over his shoulder and then they ran down the stairs with the barrel of Rail's weapon pressed against the side of Janjak's skull.

Men appeared with rifles and crazy faces.

Rail shouted "Back off!"

46

June 9
Monday Night

Teffinger dropped Rail off at the villa with a warning. "They might come for you. Get Angel to town, someplace safe." Then, with Janjak now conscious but her hands tied behind her back, he pointed the bow of the Whaler into the dark endless sea. The islands were moonlit when he got to them, taking shape a good quarter mile before he came to them.

He beached the boat on the first island, put a handcuff on Janjak's right ankle and padlocked the other end to a thirty-foot chain, which he wrapped around the base of the first palm tree he came to and secured with a second padlock. Then he cut the rope off her wrists.

There.

She wasn't going anywhere.

"You're a sexy man," she said.

"This isn't a game. Is Modeste alive?"

"For now."

"Where is she?"

"Her body or her soul?"

Teffinger kneeled down until his face was close to hers. "Here's the way this is going to work. I'm going to hand you a cell phone and you're going to call your men and tell them to release her. Once she's someplace safe, I'll take you back and then we'll all go our separate ways. If you don't make the call, I'll find her myself and you can rot here while I do."

The woman ran her fingers through Teffinger's hair.

"You like my back, don't you? You want to touch it again—"

Teffinger stood up, looked down at her for a second, and then headed back to the Whaler for food and water and blankets, trying to harden his heart with each passing step by reminding himself that a lot of good people were dead because of her. Station, for starters; and probably Poppy. Plus, she'd somehow gotten her fangs into Kovi-Ke and turned her into a killer. Not to mention that her men tried to kill him; and even though they didn't succeed, they made him throw a bottle into one of their faces, a fact that he'd have to live with in relative secrey for the rest of his life.

Those were just the things he knew about.

They were probably less than one percent, given the way the island was so terrified of her.

She deserved to die.

No one would miss her.

The world would be a better place.

Still, could he personally do it?

Could he actually let her rot to death?

The answer surprised him.

If it came down to either Modeste or Janjak dying, it wouldn't be Modeste.

When he returned, Janjak was dancing in the sand with her

top off and her arms up, as if not having a care in the world.

Teffinger took a seat out of reach and watched.

Her movements resonated in the deep recesses of his brain. He was wired for them. His eyes were always on the hunt for them. His loins were always ready for them. His tongue was always ready to taste them.

"Do you like me?"

"No."

She laughed.

"Liar."

To prove herself right, she unwrapped her skirt and threw it at him. Under it, she wore nothing. Her body gyrated under the moonlight and her hands played in the air above her head.

"How about now? Do you like me now?"

"This won't work," he said.

A minute passed.

"Take me," she said. "Take me and after you do, I'll make that call you want. You can have your precious little Modeste back. I'll leave her alone."

He knew a trick when he saw one.

"No thanks."

"Do it now, right now, otherwise I'm going to close my eyes and kill her."

He grunted.

"That's not possible."

"Mark the time," she said.

Then she laid down on her back on the sand, got her body perfectly still, and closed her eyes.

A second passed, then another and another and another. Teffinger's brain exploded with uncertainty. Could the woman really do it? Was there any chance she actually had powers?

He went over and kneeled at her side.

"Stop," he said.

She opened her eyes.

"Take me. Do it slowly," she said. "Take your time."

"If I do you'll set her free?"

"Yes. There are no tricks."

"I want you to stay away from Rail, too," he said.

"He's not part of the deal. Take me or don't, your choice."

She raised her arms above her head.

Against his will, almost as if being pulled by a force, Teffinger put a hand on the woman's stomach. It was warm. It trembled under his touch.

"You love me," she said.

"I love you."

"Show me how much you love me."

His hands went to her breasts, her tiny but oh so compelling breasts. He could feel his touch go straight through the woman's body and into her brain.

"You love me," she said.

"I love you."

Those were words he hadn't said in a long, long time. When they came out, he at first thought he was playing along, placating her, saying and doing whatever it took to free Modeste.

Then he realized that he meant them.

He meant them with every molecule in his body.

He loved her with everything he had and then ten times more.

She kissed him on the mouth.

"We'll be together forever," she said.

"Yes."

"This is our beginning."

"Yes."

"We'll never end."

"No, never."

His hands explored her body, her erotic little body, memorizing her curves and her reactions and her skin. He had never wanted a woman so badly in his life.

Kovi-Ke had been a mistake.

Evil Angel had been a mistake.

Every woman he'd ever met had been a mistake.

He realized that now, only too clearly.

He'd been born for her.

She'd been born for him.

"Unchain me," she said.

He did.

Then he flipped her over and licked her back. Sand worked its way into his mouth and he didn't care. He licked her, again and again, feeling the scars under the touch of his tongue, even the one he'd laid in. It tasted right. It tasted like there was nothing else left in the world, only this, only right here, only right now, only her and him, so perfect together, reinventing time and everything else in the universe.

DAY SEVEN

June 10
Tuesday

47

June 10
Tuesday Morning

Teffinger woke Tuesday morning and immediately realized that the sun was high and that the break of dawn had long since passed. He didn't remember a single dream or shifting even one time during the night. It was as if he'd been dead.

He was naked.

His cloths were to the side.

His body ached from the hardness of the sand.

His brain flashed with images; images of Janjak dancing in the moonlight, of him licking the woman's back and then flipping her over and taking her with every fiber of his being.

Janjak wasn't next to him.

He bolted to his feet.

"Janjak!"

No one answered.

She wasn't there.

His eyes darted to the Whaler to find it gone. He ran to the water's edge and looked in all directions. The woman was nowhere in sight, not up or down, not across on one of the other islands, not anywhere.

She was as gone as the night.

He dropped down right where he was, in a foot of water, and felt as if he'd been punched in the stomach. The woman had tricked him. He didn't care about that. What he did care about is that she'd abandoned him.

His lover had left without saying goodbye.

There was nothing worse in the world.

Nothing.

He put his clothes on.

The cell phone wasn't in his pocket; the ten coins too, were missing.

The food and water were still left.

He could live for a week.

That was something.

Rail and Angel knew he was here.

They'd come for him sooner or later.

There was no need to panic.

Well, that wasn't a hundred percent true. It was more accurate to say that there was no need to panic assuming that Rail and Angel were still alive.

Frankly, at this point, he wasn't sure he cared.

Janjak had left him.

He'd finally met the woman he was destined to be with and she threw him away.

He was nothing more than an old rag.

He wandered up and down the beach, pacing for over an hour, kicking up the water and cursing himself for not controlling his own fate. He didn't know if it was because of the sun or the motion or just the passage of time, but his head slowly began to clear. Step by step he fell out of love with Janjak and increasingly recognized her for what she was.

How did she manipulate him so thoroughly last night?

Sure, she was seductive and the moonlight was just right, but that shouldn't have been enough to make him so completely lose his senses.

Suddenly an image flashed, an image of Janjak and him digging in the sand in the middle of the night, intent on recovering something buried under the ground.

The coins?

Did he tell her about the coins?

No, he couldn't have.

Why would he?

Yet, the image was intense.

He surveyed the third island, two hundred yards away, with an eye to whether he could swim that far given his battered state.

It didn't matter.

He had to know.

He stripped his clothes off, waded out until he was waist deep and then went into a slow, overhand stroke, not setting any records but eventually coming out the other side alive.

When he got to where the coins were buried, there was nothing but an empty hole.

He slumped down with his back against a palm.

Why did he tell Janjak about it?

Did he tell her about Evil Angel having the other half?

48

June 10
Tuesday Afternoon

An hour passed, then another and another. Noon came and went. No boats broke the horizon. No one came for Teffinger. The island sat alone and desolate in its own eerie silence, interrupted only by the gentle lapping of the water against the beach and the occasional squawk of a seagull or the rustle of a palm.

Teffinger was no longer part of the world.

He was irrelevant.

He was invisible.

There was a good chance Rail and Angel were dead. They would have called early this morning to check on him and not gotten an answer; or gotten an answer from Janjak. They would have had plenty of time to rent another boat and get out here to check on things.

Suddenly it happened.

The shape of a boat broke the horizon, hardly more than a dot at this distance but kicking up enough spray to frame it as an actual vessel approaching at some speed.

It came straight for the island.

The silhouette of one person slowly took shape.

Then it took the shape of Janjak.

Her dreadlocks bounced in sync with the boat.

She wore no top.

Down below was a wrap-around skirt.

She trimmed the outboards up as she came to the beach and then hopped over the edge into knee-deep water as the bow planted itself in the sand.

She had no gun or obvious weapon.

"You have a lot of guts coming back here," Teffinger said.

She walked past him towards the palms and said over her shoulder, "Your prize is in the boat."

He checked.

Modeste was on the floor near the stern, lying on her stomach, either dead or unconscious. He jumped in to find her breathing, alive. Her face and body were battered but not any worse than the last time he'd seen her.

"Bring her up here," Janjak shouted.

Teffinger complied, carrying the woman across the beach up to the palms and laying her softly on the sand in the shade. She didn't respond much, obviously drugged.

"What'd you give her?"

Janjak approached, ran her fingers through Teffinger's hair and looked deep into his eyes. "You're the first person I'd had in a long, long time."

"That wasn't the question."

She kissed him on the lips.

He had time to pull back but didn't, or couldn't, or both.

She kissed him again and he responded.

She whispered in his ear, "I found the diamonds."

"What diamonds?"

She rubbed her stomach against his.

"You know."

"I told you about them?"

"Yes."

"Why?"

"You had no choice," she said.

"Even if I did, there's no way you could have found them," he said. "All I would have been able to tell you is the general location."

"I looked through your eyes."

"What's that mean?"

"It means I found them," she said. "Modeste is in something you might call a nether land, between life and death. I can push her either way any time I want, or just leave her there until her body consumes itself."

"Prove it. Bring her back right now."

She stepped back and ran a finger down his chest.

"First we dig."

"I don't get it."

"Sure you do, under that second pile of bones you told me about, on the other island. Don't worry about Modeste. She'll be fine."

They hopped over on the Whaler, scattered the bones to the side and then dug, shallow at first, then deeper and then even deeper, past where Teffinger had to go before, and found nothing, not a single coin, not an old belt buckle, not a rusty dagger, nothing.

Janjak sank to the ground.

Her face twisted with disappointment.

"I was going to let this be your final act. I was just going to go away and not worry about what Evil Angel has. Now there's a difference to make up." She saw the doubt on

Teffinger's face and said, "You told me about Evil Angel's half of the dig. I want those coins; I want them by tonight. Then I'll bring Modeste back to life. She'll live and so will you."

Teffinger kicked the sand.

"You have the diamonds, they're worth ten times more than the coins, maybe a hundred," he said. "Let's just end it where it is."

The woman grabbed Teffinger's hand and led him towards the boat, saying, "That reminds me, there's one diamond missing—Marilyn. I want that one too, by tonight, with the coins."

"I don't have it."

"Yeah, I know, you told me. Constance has it. Get it from her."

Teffinger hated himself.

What else had he told the woman?

"I don't know where she is."

"Find her," Janjak said. "Because if I have to find her myself, well, let's just say that she'd wish you had instead."

Teffinger stopped and put a serious expression on his face.

"I'm half tempted to just kill you right where you stand."

The woman backed up two steps, hiked her skirt up and squared off.

"Come on," she said. "Do it."

Teffinger's chest pounded.

He was tired of playing games.

He was through with all of it.

It needed to end.

It needed to end right now.

He took a deep breath and charged.

49

June 10
Tuesday Afternoon

Teffinger charged, committing every muscle in his body to the assault, only to have Janjak sidestep at the last second. All his might pounded into thin air, causing him to lose his balance and slam chest first into the wet sand at the water's edge.

"Come on! Kill me!"

He charged again, intent on getting an iron grip on anything he could and then bringing her down.

The woman twisted and swung a lightning kick at his chest, smashing his lungs with an evil force and knocking his air into oblivion.

He gasped for breath.

Then he charged again.

The woman shifted to the right but he anticipated it and caught her by the arm as she swung a fist at his face. She fell backwards into the water.

He was on her with a viper's speed, straddling her chest and pushing her shoulders down.

Her head went under water, not far, not more than six

inches, but enough.

She twisted violently.

He didn't let up, not for a scary long time, and then at the last second he jerked her head up as she gasped wildly for breath.

She landed a fist to the side of his face.

"Kill me! Do it!"

He pushed her back under, feeling every molecule of her body trying to free itself from his horrible grasp. Her face was crystal clear. The terror in her eyes arced through the water and straight into Teffinger's brain.

Something deep in his being snapped.

Don't!

Don't!

Don't!

He jerked her head up, stared at her in disbelief as she coughed up water, and then got off and stood up. The woman eased up on to her elbows and let the wisp of a victory smile come to her lips.

He walked over to the Whaler and pushed it off the sand.

It rocked gently in the water.

"Come on," he said. "We're done here."

Silently, they motored over to where Modeste was. To Teffinger's distress, she was in the exact position and the exact state of unconsciousness as they'd left her.

Janjak approached him, carefully, and put her lips to his.

"You've earned this," she said. "I'm going to wake her. Get her ready—put her on her back, face up. There's a machete on the boat under the front seat. Get it for me, I'm going to need it. Oh, your cell phone is there too, by the way."

With that, the woman disappeared into the palms.

Five minutes later, she returned dangling a large nasty green snake from her left hand. The reptile repeatedly jerked its body and swung its head at Janjak's legs, trying to sink its fangs into her flesh but always falling short.

The woman dangled the snake over Modeste's face, not more than six inches off, then swung it back and forth again and again and again.

Then she lopped off its head with the machete.

She let the blood and guts drip onto Modeste's face.

Ten seconds later the woman abruptly woke with a start.

Janjak tossed the snake's body to the side and said to Teffinger, "Take the Whaler and go. Make no mistake that what I just did doesn't affect tonight. I still want the other diamond—Marilyn—by tonight. I also want Evil Angel's coins, by tonight. If I don't get them, I'll put your little friend here right back where I got her from; and I'll be giving her a lot of company, you included."

Teffinger helped Modeste to her feet then squared off against Janjak.

"Where do I meet you?"

"Right here."

"I'll be back, one way or the other."

"Until darkness comes," she said. "That's how long you have. Until darkness comes. Not a minute more."

"Like I said, I'll be back."

The woman grabbed him by the arm and jerked him to a stop as he turned for the Whaler.

"You need to learn how to kill," she said. "It's your only weakness."

"Maybe you can teach me someday."

"Maybe I will."

50

June 10
Tuesday Afternoon

Rhythmically cutting through calm blue seas away from the island, totally and wonderfully free of Janjak, Teffinger let himself take a deep breath and savor the moment.

The sun was a taste of love on his face.

The wind in his hair was a woman's touch.

The vessel gently lifted and fell with a playful rhythm.

Modeste was fine.

She was safe, right there next to him.

Teffinger filled her in on the last few days.

She remembered being captured and beaten in an effort to force her to disclose what she'd done with the diamonds and gold, and then falling into an eerie, ghostly world of shadows and fears, where she stayed until she suddenly awoke just a short time ago.

"If I were you, I'd get on the first airplane out of here and never come back," Teffinger said.

The woman shook her head.

"No!"

"Look—"

"We need to give her what she wants," she said. "I can't go back to that place!"

"It's not real," Teffinger said. "You were drugged or something."

"It's not real? It's as real as the sky over our heads."

Teffinger frowned.

"I'll make a deal with you," he said. "You get on the first plane out of here so I don't have to worry about you any more, and I'll take care of Janjak."

"How?"

"I don't know, but I will."

Her face wrinkled with stress.

"She's inside me. I can feel her. She's like a worm slithering around in my soul. Going somewhere isn't going to help."

"You haven't eaten for days," he said. "Your mind's playing tricks. Just do what I say. I'm going to put you on a plane, you're going to get out of here, and I'm going to take care of everything."

The woman looked doubtful.

"Are you going to kill her?"

"No."

"Then you won't be taking care of her."

"Just let me handle it."

"She has to die. That's the only way this can end. She has to die."

51

June 10
Tuesday Afternoon

There was a good chance Rail would kill Modeste for stealing his stuff and setting all the ugliness in motion. She knew it all too well and didn't argue when Teffinger holed her up in a seedy hotel in Port-au-Prince to await further instructions.

Back at the villa Rail and Angel were alive and well but that was where the good news ended. After hearing everything that had transpired, they quickly reached the same conclusion as Modeste.

"Janjak needs to die."

They weren't interested in letting her keep what she already had, much less giving her more.

"Screw her and her stupid voodoo," Rail said. "If I don't get those diamonds back, I'm a dead man."

"Count me out," Teffinger said.

Rail hardened his face.

"Fine, you're out," he said. "You know what? In hindsight I'm sorry I ever pulled your sorry ass out of the ocean. I can't believe you were sitting on my diamonds the whole time and never told me. What were you going to do? Retire on them?"

"No."

"No?"

"No. I was saving them as a bargaining chip to get Modeste back if everything else failed. I was hoping to get her back without having to use them and then give them back to you. Everyone would have won."

"Well, that's not the way it worked out, is it?"

"Apparently not."

"You know what? Get out of here."

Teffinger looked at Angel.

Her face was as defiant as Rail's.

"You heard him," she said. "Get out."

Rail called a guard and said, "Give him a ride to town." Then to Teffinger, "Have a nice trip. You know what? As long as we're talking about hindsight, in hindsight I wouldn't have shot that guy back at Janjak's place. You know the one I'm talking about, right? The one who was beating you to death? In hindsight, I should have just let him do his thing." He shook his head with disgust. "I save your sorry little ass—twice! And in return, what do you do? You give my diamonds—the diamonds I needed to stay alive—you give them to some screwed up voodoo witch, who by the way you end up banging, literally hours after Evil Angel gave you her heart and soul. Get out of here and piss back to Denver or wherever the hell it is that you came from."

Angel spit at Teffinger's feet.

It hit his shoe.

He didn't wipe it off.

He turned and left.

52

June 10
Tuesday Afternoon

In Port-au-Prince, Modeste was gone when Teffinger checked on her. There was no sign of a struggle. The guy at the register confirmed she'd left of her own volition, "more than two hours ago, in a hurry, man, in a big old hurry." The words were a punch to Teffinger's gut. After all he went through to save her, when she probably didn't even deserve it to start with, now she was out there somewhere throwing it all away, probably chasing down some stupid plan to kill Janjak.

So be it.

Ten minutes down the street he found a place that sold cell phones, bought two, and called Sydney as he walked towards the ocean side of the city.

"What's the status on your end?"

"Teffinger?"

"Yeah."

"We've had three homicides in the last 24 hours," she said. "Your being AWOL was the breaking point for the chief. He wanted me to tell you if you called that there's no need to rush back."

"I'm coming back tomorrow. I have one more thing to wrap up tonight and then I'm done here."

"Teff, listen to what I'm saying. We're all reporting to Richardson now. The email went out to everyone yesterday. Have you checked your messages?"

"No."

"Well, do it, because it's there."

"Yeah, yeah, I'll check. Have you had any luck finding Kovi-Ke?"

"No. The earth swallowed her."

"Figures. I'll be back tomorrow."

"I have your personal things in my office," she said.

"Robertson's already moved into mine?"

"Yes."

"He sure didn't waste any time, did he?"

"Nick, you need to take this seriously. You're not going to walk back into the chief's office and smooth it all out like you've done before. This time is different. It's real this time."

"Well, maybe I won't come back, then. Maybe I'll just stay down here."

The woman sighed.

"I tried to warn you ten different times."

"I got to go."

He hung up, dialed Kovi-Ke's dive shop in Jamaica and got greeted by a deep, male voice.

"Is Kovi-Ke there?"

"No."

"Do you know when she'll be back?"

"Not really. Can I take a message?"

"Tell her Teffinger called," he said.

"Teffinger?"

"Right, Teffinger. Nick Teffinger."

"I'll tell her."

"Wait, let me give you my number. Have her call me as soon as she shows up. You got a pencil?"

"Yeah, give it to me."

Five minutes down the street something happened he didn't expect—Rail's lawyer was across the street talking to a flirty woman in a short red dress, obviously for sale. They looked like they were negotiating price. By her smile and constant touch, she was convincing him she'd be worth it.

What was the guy's name?

Stephen something.

Blake, that was it; Stephen Blake, out of New York.

Teffinger headed over and pulled the man to the side.

"Your client Johnnie Rail is planning on killing someone."

"Who?"

"A voodoo woman. Her name's Janjak."

"How do you know?"

"He told me."

"So what do you want me to do?"

"Talk him out of it."

"You're kidding, right? You don't talk Johnnie out of anything."

Teffinger frowned.

"What are you still doing in town?"

The man nodded towards the woman.

"What's it look like?"

"Well, have fun."

"I intend to."

Teffinger left.

Two steps later he turned and said, "Do you have a pencil?"

"A pen."

"Write down my number," he said. "Give it to Rail when you talk to him. Tell him to call me."

He rented a 30-foot Baja go-fast with twin big-blocks and made a beeline for the islands. The money was insane but the vessel was twice as fast as the Whaler, should that ever become an issue.

The engines spit rumble for two miles so it wasn't a surprise to spot Janjak waiting for him on the beach as he motored up and let the bow kiss the sand.

The sun was losing its heat.

The shadows were long.

The woman was the same as when he'd left her, topless up above and barefoot down below, with a wrap-around skirt separating the two.

"You're early," she said.

"Johnnie Rail's coming to kill you," he said. "I came to get you out of here."

"I thought you and Rail were working together."

"We parted ways," Teffinger said. "Those diamonds you dug up, Rail stole them from some guy in Hong Kong. The guy's closing in on him and he needs to be in a position to give them back. Getting them back starts with killing you."

The woman put her arms around Teffinger's neck and pressed her stomach to his.

"So, why don't you just let him?"

"Because I want you to leave Modeste alone," he said.

"Whatever you owe me for getting you out of here, I want you to pay it to Modeste by leaving her alone. Whatever you and Rail end up doing to each other, I just don't want Modeste dragged into it."

The woman kissed him.

"Modeste wants to kill me too," she said.

Teffinger shifted his feet, not knowing how the woman knew that but convinced that somehow she did.

"She just wants to be alive and not have to worry about being pulled into some nether world," he said. "It's a self-defense thing. Once she knows you're going to leave her alone, it'll all be over. Rail wants to kill her too for stealing his stuff in the first place, so she'll be leaving Haiti, she'll have no choice. You'll never hear from her again."

"Are you in love with her?"

He shook his head.

"Anything but," he said. "In fact she played me from the start."

"So why do you want to help her?"

"I don't know," he said. "Look, this Hong Kong guy is eventually going to hone in on Rail. From there it won't be too hard to figure out where the diamonds went next, to you. So even if you kill Rail, you'll still have the Hong Kong guy to worry about. This thing is never going to end. You got the coins. Keep them and cut your losses."

"Give the diamonds back to Rail?"

"Yes, either him or directly back to the Hong Kong guy. I'll help you find out who he is if you want to go in that direction. Maybe Rail can convince Angel to hand her coins over to you as a gesture of good will. Whether that happens or not, you'll still be in a position where you won't have to look over your shoulder for the rest of your life."

A seagull swept low over the water, silently hunting for unsuspecting prey.

Two more followed.

"Let's get out of here," Teffinger said. "Rail could be showing up at any minute."

The woman raised her arms above her head and twirled in an erotic dance.

Then she suddenly stopped and looked hard at Teffinger.

"Modeste's destiny lies in her own hands," she said. "I want that final diamond. I want it by tonight. She can get it. That's how she gets away from me. That's the only way she gets away from me. So, either kill me yourself, right here right now, or go tell her."

"I don't know where she is. She took off."

"Then she dies at midnight."

She ripped her skirt off, threw it to the side and waded into the water. Waist deep she turned and said, "The clock's ticking."

Then she dived in and went into an overhand stroke in the direction of the other island.

Teffinger watched her for a minute, then fired up the Baja and got the hell out of there.

53

June 10
Tuesday Evening

Back in the city, Teffinger's initial plan was to step aside from all the craziness, go to a bar, get drunk, pick up a woman and screw her all the way to morning. The specter of Station's murder, though, wouldn't leave him alone. She'd died because Teffinger hadn't been smart enough to stay in town.

He'd made a promise to himself to not let the same thing happen to Modeste.

Station had deserved his help.

Modeste didn't, not really, at least not more than Teffinger had already given her. Technically, he'd fulfilled any promise he'd made to her, or to himself.

But, still.

He dialed the Like a Virgin pretty, Constance.

"It's me, Teffinger," he said. "Are you in Haiti?"

"No, New York."

"Where's the diamond?"

A pause, then, "I can't tell you."

"Why not?"

"Because Modeste told me not to."

"When?"

"An hour ago," she said.

"Modeste isn't thinking clearly," he said. "I need that diamond and I need it now. Tomorrow's too late."

"Sorry, she gave me instructions."

"If you don't tell me, she's going to be dead by midnight."

"I'm sorry."

The line died.

He dialed back.

She didn't answer.

He stomped off blindly, not caring where he was going, simply feeding the need to be in motion.

The street buzzed with traffic.

Buildings passed.

"Where's the diamond?"

A pause, then, "I can't tell you."

The words kept playing in his head.

"Where's the diamond?"

A pause, then, "I can't tell you."

There was something wrong with them. Two blocks passed before he figured out what it was. If the diamond was with Constance she would have said, "I have it," or "It's with me," or words to that effect.

She didn't say she had it though. She said, "I can't tell you."

She didn't have it, not with her, anyway.

She must have stashed it somewhere before she left Haiti.

Where? Her apartment?

Teffinger called her again, this time from his other phone. "Don't hang up, don't hang up," he said. "Just listen. Give me one minute. Don't hang up."

"There's nothing you can say."

"Consider this," he said. "Do you remember when you gave me all the other diamonds but held onto Marilyn? Do you remember what you told me about why you wanted to hang onto her?"

"No."

"You said, She's a final bargaining chip, in case you get killed or taken. Do you remember that?"

A pause, then, "Yes, but that's not valid anymore. You got Modeste. She's free. You don't need anything as a bargaining chip."

"Listen to what I say and listen carefully," he said. "Modeste is going to die tonight. She doesn't know it yet, because I haven't been able to find her and tell her, but that's what's going to happen. I need that diamond to keep her alive. If she knew she was going to die, she'd tell you to tell me where it is. If you don't believe me, call her and then call me back."

An hour later he was in the Baja with the diamond in his pocket, storming through choppy waters with the throttle at redline and the go-fast's bow jarring up and down to a demonic beat.

His gut churned.

This could all be a setup.

Janjak might kill everyone as soon as she had the diamond, first Teffinger, right then and there, and then Modeste.

He had to keep his guard up.

He had to do this right.

He had to watch her every move.

She was a she-devil, one with hypnotic moments, but a

she-devil nonetheless, and that was true based only on the things she'd admitted to—Kovi-Ke, Station, and all the rest.

She was evil.

He couldn't forget that, not for a second.

He couldn't let her get her spell on him, not again.

54

June 10
Tuesday Evening

An ominous twilight thickened quickly over the Haitian waters. The Baja was a wild beast, deafening in its roar and frantic in its motions. It didn't slow until the islands appeared up ahead as black silhouettes against an almost-black sky. Teffinger motored into the thick of it to find something he didn't expect. Three boats were at the beach. One was the Whaler. The others were similar in size.

Teffinger hung back in neutral, eyeing the situation.

No one shot at him.

He killed the engines so he could hear.

No sounds came from shore.

No lights flashed.

No signs of life emerged.

He brought the vessel in and hopped off the bow into knee-deep water. A lifeless, dark silhouette appeared in the sand up ahead. An inspection showed it to be a body, a very dead body with a large bloody wound to the side of the head. Teffinger nudged it with his foot and got no response. Next to the body was a rifle. He picked it up, checked the action and looked around.

There was enough light to show a vertical person if one was there to see.

There wasn't.

He walked down the beach. A light breeze blew. The moon was full and throwing enough light down to create shadows. Teffinger's shadow moved ahead him like some kind of eerie attachment.

He came across another body, very similar to the first except this one had massive wounds to the forearms in addition to the face.

Teffinger nudged it, not expecting a response and not getting one.

He kept moving.

In the next four minutes he found four more bodies, all the same, all hacked to death. He recognized three of them as Rail's men. One was the guy who drove Teffinger to town this afternoon.

A motion caught his peripheral vision. It was Janjak, forty or fifty yards away, walking towards him with a large knife or machete in her right hand.

She didn't call out.

Teffinger swallowed and then walked towards her.

Two steps later he stumbled upon another body in the sand.

The man's face was sliced in two.

55

June 10
Tuesday Night

Teffinger and Janjak stopped three steps short of one another.

Teffinger said, "Did you kill all these men?"

"Yes."

"By yourself?"

"Yes."

"How?"

"I have my ways. They came here to kill me. That was a mistake." She walked to him, dropped the machete in the sand, put her arms around his neck and whispered in his ear, "Did you bring the diamond?"

His instinct was to play coy, to not give her a concrete answer, to hedge his bets. His tongue didn't obey his instinct.

He dropped the rifle and said, "Yes."

She kissed him.

"Good. Follow me."

"Where's Rail?"

"I'll show you later."

She picked up the machete and headed for the palms.

Teffinger reached for the rifle.

"Leave it," Janjak said. "You don't need it."

She led him to the bones, the ones he and Evil Angel found the coins under, and started pushing the pile to the side.

"Help me."

He hesitated, not knowing her game, and then joined in.

They cleared the bones and skulls away from the center and then dug a hole, deeper and deeper, until it was at least five feet down.

"Good enough."

Janjak reached into the shadows and pulled out Teffinger's old shirt, the one he'd initially used to hold the coins, the one he'd buried on the other island, the one he told Janjak about but didn't know why. She opened it up, dangled it over the hole and let the coins drop in, falling on one another with a metallic banging. Then she tossed the shirt to the side and said, "Give me the diamond."

He pulled it out of his pocket and held it out.

She checked it, made sure it was real, and then tossed it in.

"I don't get it," Teffinger said.

"Maybe some day I'll explain."

They filled the hole in, stomped it down and moved the bones back into position.

"Do one more thing and then Modeste is free," the woman said. "Constance too, and you too for that matter. The last thing I want you to do is bring all the bodies from the beach over here and throw them on the pile."

Teffinger envisioned it.

They'd be heavy.

It would take some time.

Their blood would get all over him.

"That's it then, right? That's the final thing?"

"Yes."

"What about Evil Angel?"

"I have no need for her any more," Janjak said. "The diamond made up for her coins. I don't need them any more."

"So she's free?"

"Yes."

Teffinger set to it.

It took him more than forty painful and repugnant minutes but he got it done.

"Follow me," Janjak said. "I'll show you Rail."

Teffinger braced.

They hadn't parted friends, but the man had saved his life, twice, once from the lonely clutches of the sea, and then from being beaten to death by Janjak's men.

Janjak walked ahead of him, saying nothing, dangling the machete from her right hand.

Teffinger followed with a beating chest.

He could feel the grim reaper walking next to him.

He already knew how it would end. The woman would tighten her curse over him so he wouldn't be able to resist.

She'd play with him a little, giving him a kiss or maybe even seducing him fully under the moonlight, one final time.

Then she'd raise the brutal blade of the machete high over her head with both arms and swing it down into his face with every muscle of her being.

She'd drag him onto the bones, just one more sucker for the pile.

Then she'd be gone with one more story to tell over cocktails.

56

June 10
Tuesday Night

Rail wasn't dead but instead was staked out in the sand with a gag in his mouth and wild demons in his eyes. "Teffinger's here," Janjak said.

Rail struggled wildly against his bonds.

Frantic unintelligible sounds came from his mouth.

Teffinger's instinct was to knock the machete out of Janjak's hand, overcome her and free Rail. Before he could finalize the decision and act, though, the woman waved the weapon at him and said, "Stay back!"

He forced himself to not charge.

Keeping Teffinger at bay, the woman slit her wrist and let the blood drip down onto Rail's face and into his eyes. He twisted and contorted as if it was acid. Then the woman dropped the machete, walked to Teffinger and held her wrist out.

"Drink," she said. "This is my gift to you."

It was crazy.

Teffinger knew he should resist.

He should punch her.

He should knock her out.

Instead he pulled her wrist to his mouth and drank.

Instantly everything changed.

A vision was in his head, a vision so real it was as if he was actually there.

It was a hot, humid, Miami night. Across the street was a lesbian bar called Blackbird Ordinary. He waited across the street in his car waiting for the right little bitch to step out; sufficiently drunk, sufficiently pretty, sufficiently blond, sufficiently parked far enough away from random eyes.

He checked his face in the rearview mirror.

It was pretty.

His hair was long and black and thick.

His eyes were green.

Everything about him said rock star.

The wait wasn't long, no more than five minutes.

That's how fast the perfect woman emerged, beautifully alone, beautifully tipsy, beautifully appearing before his eyes as if sent for his amusement. He did a 180 and pulled to a stop next to her just as she was opening her car door. He powered down the passenger window, leaned over and flashed his best smile.

"Excuse me but I'm a bit lost."

The words came with a hypnotic English accent. They came from a perfect face framed with perfect hair. She was already his, lesbian or not. He chatted her up and then sealed the deal by letting it drop oh-so-innocently that he was someone named Johnnie Rail, a rock god from England.

"Busted Skies," he said. "That's our latest song. Have you ever heard it?"

"Are you kidding? I love it!"

"I wasn't sure how good it was doing over here in the states," he said. "In London it's been number one for six weeks."

They chatted.

Her name was Alley Savannah.

Thirty minutes later he had her on the ground on her back, dead, stabbed in the back of the neck. Her pulled up her blouse and let her perfect little stomach show, so beautiful. It wasn't moving, the way it would be if she were breathing. It was totally and absolutely still. That was the best part about it, the way it was so incredibly still.

With a pencil, he wrote, 1 6 Weeks on a piece of paper. He did it in block lettering, not his normal handwriting, real slow, forcing himself to not use his usual writing. He folded the paper until it was only about two inches long. Then he rolled it up until it was shaped like a cigarette and put it inside a glass vial about three inches long. He screwed the cap on. Then he cut a slit in the woman's stomach and shoved the vial in.

"Bye-bye, Alley Savannah."

The vision disappeared, everything turned black for a few seconds as if 8mm reels were being changed out, followed by a new vision with a new excitement and a new thirsty need to kill.

The second murder involved Jaylor Colt, technically a Cuban diplomat in Washington, D.C., but that night nothing more than a sweet little piece of salsa ass.

More reels followed.

Faren White.

Jackie Vampire.

And Nicole Carter, a San Francisco attorney, whose throat

needed to be slit and finally was, down at the BNSF switch-yard next to Tarzan's place.

The visions stopped.

Teffinger sprang back into his own brain.

Rail was the killer.

The eyes that Kovi-Ke had been seeing through belonged to Johnnie Rail.

Teffinger's blood raced.

Could it be proved in court? Maybe, if there was physical evidence tying Rail to the scene, but to Teffinger's knowledge, there was none. Even if there was, by the time they got an arrest warrant, Rail would be long gone, living the life of a rock star in some country that had no extradition.

He looked at Janjak.

"You knew this? You knew Rail was the killer I was looking for?"

"Yes and I know a lot more, a whole lot more," she said. "But first it's time for him to die. His time is over."

She picked up the machete.

Rail pulled wildly at the ropes.

It did no good.

"You can do it if you want," Janjak told Teffinger. "If you don't do it, I will."

Twenty seconds later the deadly blade of the machete sliced into Rail's face, through the bone and deep into his brain. He gurgled for a second and then his head tilted to the side and every part of his body stopped moving.

TWO MONTHS LATER

August 10
Tuesday

57

August 10
Tuesday Afternoon

In the flesh, through the window of the taxi, Ugly Tuna Diving Adventures wasn't exactly what Teffinger expected. In his mind, he'd built it up to something pretty special, something that would scream to tourists with the pitch-perfect voice of a postcard. The ragged reality was that it sat near the commercial and fishing docks of Montego Bay, the sign above the door was hand-painted wood, and the structure was small and weathered.

Teffinger stepped out the cab, thanked the driver with a generous tip and got his bearings.

The Jamaican sun was high and bright.

The waters were the same color as the sky but a slightly deeper hue.

Seagulls were everywhere.

The docks and channels were alive with boats and activity and commotion that seemed to stretch forever.

He felt as if he was on another planet.

His heart raced.

Kovi-Ke didn't know he was coming.

He hadn't told her.

He hadn't had the guts.

He had no suitcase, he had no hotel reservation, he had nothing but the blood cruising hot through his veins and the hope that he hadn't come all this way for nothing.

He took a deep breath, pulled the aluminum screen door open and stepped inside. Reggae music greeted him from crackly speakers but that was all.

No one was there.

"Anyone home?"

No one answered.

"Hello?"

A rotating desk fan blew into his face and then away.

A wooden door at the back of the structure was wedged open with a brick. Teffinger went through it and found himself on a large dock; piers, planks, ropes, tires, seagulls, a boatyard in the distance with a hundred or more sailboats on blocks—they raked his peripheral vision. His primary vision focused on the woman ten steps away with her back to him, doing something with a dive tank, possibly fixing it or replacing a component. A toolbox was at her side. She wore a white tank top, dampened with sweat. Pink shorts played nicely against shapely mocha legs. Her hair was pulled into a ponytail. The strands at the back of her neck were damp and stuck against her skin. Black flip-flips protected her feet from splinters.

Teffinger stayed quiet, watching her work, mesmerized by the movement of her muscles and the way she wiped the sweat off her brow with the back of her hand.

When she finally detected his presence and turned, her chest heaved and her eyes widened.

"Teffinger?"

He nodded.

"Yes."

"I look terrible."

"Not from where I'm standing."

"What are you doing here?"

"I came for a kiss. Do you have any spare ones laying around that you're not using?"

She smiled.

"I might."

She took him inside the shop, shut and locked the doors, flipped the sign to Closed, pulled the blinds, turned up the music and got all over him with her hands and her lips and her legs and her thighs and her tongue and her nasty little moves.

He responded with every fiber of his being, giving as good as he got.

He was an addict.

She was the drug.

The touch of her skin was more than he remembered. The months had made her fade in spite of the constant thoughts he'd thrown her way. Now she was back, refilling his soul and giving him a reason to live, a reason to die and a reason to be everything in-between.

They took their fill of one another.

For Teffinger, it was more than sex.

It was more than just the incredible dance of the woman's body against him.

It was more than just this moment.

It was more than just the past.

It was more.

It was more.

It was forever more.

He didn't know exactly what happened inside him, or why it happened, but he did know it had happened and that he would never be the same, not in ten minutes, not in ten hours, not in ten years.

He was a different man now.

He was more complete.

He was more complex.

He was more vulnerable.

He was stronger.

He was weaker.

The woman had taken him to a place that he expected to exist but had never really been sure, not until now. He didn't want to be away from her; not now, not in the future, not ever.

When it was over, he rolled onto his back, caught his breath as his chest heaved and said, "I didn't come here just to see if this would happen. I also came here for business."

"What kind of business?"

"Dangerous business, I'm afraid."

58

August 10
Tuesday Afternoon

They ended up sitting in a shady area of the dock behind the shop, dangling their feet over the water. "I know we talked about this," Teffinger said, "but I want to go over it one more time before I tell you a few things. Tell me again what transpired between you and the lawyer, Stephen Blake."

"Seriously?"

"Indulge me. I'm going to be adding some parts to the story, some parts you don't know about yet, but I don't want to do that until I'm sure we're on the same page."

She held his hand.

"He showed up down here at the shop one day," she said. "I'd never seen him before. I didn't know who he was. He said he was a lawyer out of New York."

Teffinger nodded.

"Go on."

"He said he wanted to tell me something very important but that I needed to keep it confidential. Well, I couldn't say no to that, because I was too curious."

"So you agreed—"

"Right, I agreed," she said. "He told me he had a client named Johnnie Rail who was a big rock star from London. Blake did all the copywriting and related work for Rail and the band. Anyway, one day Rail mentioned something off the cuff, something that might have been illegal in some way. The lawyer was curious what was going on and sort of suckered Rail into fleshing out what he was alluding to. Well, Rail didn't, not during that particular meeting, anyway. But Rail's confidence grew over the next few meetings. And one day, when the subject sort of came up, Rail said, *When I tell you things during our meetings, it's all one hundred percent confidential and everything, right?* And the lawyer assured him it was. The lawyer was bound by law never to disclose the confidences of his client, with a few exceptions, which didn't apply to them. Plus, the lawyer was a man of his word. He promised on his mother's grave he would never tell anyone anything about Rail, and in fact never had to date. With that, Rail admitted to the lawyer that he murdered a woman; he just came flat out and said it, *I murdered a woman.* The lawyer kept his cool, pretended like it was no big deal, and got Rail to loosen his lips even more. Rail gave him all the details. The woman was someone named Alley Savannah. Rail picked her up when she came out of a lesbian bar in Miami called Blackbird Ordinary. He stabbed her in the back of the neck. Then he cut open her stomach and shoved in a vial, something like a small test tube with a cap at the end. Inside was a piece of paper that said 1 6 Weeks. What it meant is that the band's latest song, one called Baby Done Bad, had been number one on the England charts for the last six weeks." She looked into Teffinger's eyes. "Rail did kill her, right?"

"Right. It's true."

"So why are we going over this? Rail's dead—"

"You'll see in a minute. Just keep going. What else did the lawyer tell you?"

"He told me that over the next few months, Rail told him about other women he'd killed. One was named Jaylor Colt, in Washington, D.C. She actually turned out to be a Cuban diplomat although Rail didn't know it at the time. Another woman was named Faren White, in San Francisco. Another one was Lachey Silk, in New York."

"Tell me about her."

"She was a pretty blond girl," Kovi-Ke said. "She'd been out partying that evening. Rail spotted her, followed her to her apartment and got her to open the door. He got in and killed her. Then he stuck a note in a red hardcover book on the top shelf of a big bookcase that was built into the wall. The note said NOIZ. It stood for Noise, which was the name of a song the band had released the week before."

"What about someone named Jackie Vampire?"

"No."

"The lawyer never said anything about her?"

"No, Who is she?"

"She's another woman Rail killed."

"How do you know?"

"He told me about her."

"I thought he died on that voodoo island."

"He did. That's where he told me, before he died. I ran the name down. Sure enough, a woman in Chicago by that name had been murdered. The original investigators never found a note. I flew there and we took a long, hard look. We eventually found it in an air duct. It said Invasion, which was the name of a song by Rail that had just been released in the United States."

"So it was definitely him."

Teffinger nodded.

"That was one of his earlier kills, more than five years ago. He wasn't as good at covering his tracks back then. We found his fingerprints on the note and his DNA on the victim's body. He licked her nipples, probably after she was dead, but it really doesn't matter if it was before or after. That's where his DNA was."

"Well, the lawyer never mentioned her to me," Kovi-Ke said. "Rail must not have told him about that particular murder. Maybe because he was afraid there might be physical evidence there."

"That's entirely possible. Let's take a walk, do you mind?"

They stood up.

"You said you were here for business; dangerous business."

"I'm getting to it," Teffinger said. "Trust me."

"Just tell me what it is."

He hesitated and then said, "You're going to be murdered tonight."

59

August 10
Tuesday Afternoon

You're going to be murdered tonight.

She looked at Teffinger with half a grin on her face, waiting for the punch line, but it fell off when he didn't give it to her.

"Murdered by who? Janjak?"

"I'll get to that in a minute," he said. "Finish up with what you did with the lawyer. I need to be absolutely sure we're on the same page."

They walked.

Kovi-Ke composed her thoughts.

"Well, he told me that Rail had told him about all these murders in the context of an attorney-client privilege," she said. "He wasn't allowed to go to the police, even anonymously. Equally important, he'd be disbarred if he breached the privilege. The fallout would land on the firm. He'd end up penniless and railroaded out of town. But, he'd figured out a plan to avoid all that. That's where I fit in."

"How? What'd he tell you?"

"He said that Rail had a place in Haiti," she said. "He said

Rail was into voodoo and it was big in that area of the world, which is why he started sniffing around there and eventually ended up buying a villa on the sea, outside of Port-au-Prince. He became obsessed with a voodoo woman who went by the name of Janjak. They eventually formed a relationship and she started to let him come to some of the voodoo ceremonies." She looked into Teffinger's eyes and said, "Is Janjak the one who's going to murder me?"

"We're getting there. Keep going."

"Well, it got to the point where Rail wanted to see if he could develop voodoo powers," she said. "He talked Janjak into letting him pick out people to bring to the ceremonies. He talked her into letting him actually participate in the performances. During Karnaval in February of this year, Rail picked me out of the crowd and had his men confiscate me. I was taken to a beach. Janjak presided over the ceremony but Rail took over once I was staked out. He's the one who sliced open the snake and dripped the blood and guts into my face and eyes." She paused, recalling it. "Rail later told the lawyer about it. That's how the lawyer knew. The lawyer then got my name from the police report. He came to Jamaica to see me. He had a plan."

"Which was what?"

"He couldn't tell the police about any of Rail's past murders," she said. "But he could point the police to Rail when he was out to take his next victim. Rail had just concluded a tour. It was always two or three weeks after a tour that he committed his next murder. So the lawyer anticipated that the next one was looming in the near future. What he wanted me to do was to follow Rail as he zeroed in on his next victim. I would make contact with a local homicide detective and pretend I was seeing through a killer's eyes. I would in effect direct the detective to the kill that was about to take place and to Rail as the murderer. That would keep the lawyer out of the picture. It would also be plausible to Rail if he ever found out what I was doing. He could think that he'd actually done something to me during that ceremony that caused me to see out of his eyes."

"And you went along with the plan."

She nodded.

"I did. Part of it was to get a killer off the streets. A bigger part of it, though, was to get revenge. He had no right to do what he did to me. If there was any way that I could get him locked up in a little cell for the rest of his life, I was happy to give it a try. Do you understand?"

"I do, totally."

"There was a logistical issue," she said. "Obviously I couldn't really see through Rail's eyes. The lawyer had a good friend he knew from law school that he still kept in close touch with. She was a lawyer now out in San Francisco. Her name was Nicole Carter. He gave her all the background and explained his plan. What he wanted her to do was to tail Rail, watch his moves, and then feed them back to me through cell phone communications. So, all the moves that Rail was making when we weren't near him, I was able to tell you about them from a distance because Nicole was feeding them to me. It was a simple matter of checking my phone when it vibrated and not letting you see me. I'd excuse myself to go to the bathroom or something like that. As for telling you about the flashbacks, and even having them in your presence, that was all information that I had already gotten from the lawyer."

"Clever."

"Yes," she said. "It was clear that Rail's intended target was Station Smith. Of course, none of us knew why, and to tell you the truth I'm still not real clear on it, but she was the target all right."

"Let me ask you something," Teffinger said. "When we met, there was sex. Was that a way of hooking me in?"

"At first, yes."

"And later—"

"And later, we were both hooked, as I'm sure you figured out," she said. "Anyway it was all going according to plan. Obviously, though, Rail spotted Nicole at some point and that's why she ended up murdered. Since it had all gone to hell, I went into hiding." She put his hand in hers. "It's your turn to talk. Who's going to murder me tonight, and why?"

60

August 10
Tuesday Afternoon

The walk led them out of the dock area and into a small strip of bars. They ended at a back table of the Calico Jack's with bottles of beer. A large ceiling fan rotated above at minimal speed, barely enough to stir the air.

"I'm going to tell you something that I've never told a soul in the world," Teffinger said.

With that, he told her about the events on voodoo island; how Rail and his men had gone there to kill Janjak and met their fate; how he and Janjak buried the coins and the diamond under the bones; how Janjak dripped her blood into Rail's eyes and then made Teffinger suck from the wound, at which point visions of the murders played in his head; how Janjak sliced Rail's face in two with the machete; and all the rest.

"The gold and the coins were buried to re-strengthen the curse of the island," he said. "All the bones that had accumulated there over the years, they came from Janjak's ancestry. She warned me that if I ever stepped on any of the islands at any point in the future, I would die within five minutes. So if I had any notions to go back for what was buried there, I'd better get it out of my head."

"Do you believe that's true?"

He shrugged.

"I hate to admit it, but yes," he said. "Somehow she made me see through Rail's eyes. There's no way that could really happen but it did. That was on top of what happened earlier when she got me to tell her everything I didn't want her to know, and not remembering it until she told me. Plus she somehow killed all those men at close quarters. How? Some kind of mind control or curse, that's all I can figure. She has powers, how and why I don't know, but I'm not going to doubt them. I can't."

"I told you before there were rumors," she said. "That part of what I told you was true."

"Well, believe them," Teffinger said. "Here's the thing, though. She told me something very interesting. The voodoo ceremony that she performed on you, that was done at the request of the lawyer, Stephen Blake, not Rail. He chose you. He was there when it happened. He paid her for it, a lot of money."

"It wasn't Rail?"

"No, it was Blake," Teffinger said. "You weren't the first in fact. There were two others before you. After each one, he fed them the same story he fed you, about how Rail was a killer and about how he wanted them to pretend to see through Rail's eyes in an effort to bring him down. Neither of them fell for it. You did. He told you Rail was behind the ceremony so you'd want to seek revenge."

"That bastard."

"I've been doing a lot of digging over the last two months," Teffinger said. "One thing I found out is that Rail had struck up an acquaintance with a guy who used to live in Denver that we called Tarzan. I think Rail spotted Nicole Carter following him. He killed her.

"How do you know?"

"Because he flashed it for me. I think he did it Saturday morning and dumped her at Tarzan's old liar, to make it look like it was Tarzan's work. Then he boarded the first flight back to Haiti and held a big party that night, on the spur of the moment, so he'd have a lot of witnesses to verify that he was in Haiti that day."

"What about Station Smith? Who killed her?"

"Tarzan is my guess," Teffinger said. "That happened when Rail was already back in Haiti, and Tarzan's the only other person in the mix."

"But why?"

"Money."

"You think Rail paid him?"

Teffinger nodded.

"He bought himself a great big alibi. Someone was following Station. Then, *bam*, she gets murdered when Rail is clearly in Haiti, meaning he's just some innocent guy wandering the earth like the rest of us."

"But why bother killing her at all?"

"My guess? Because he pictured her dead too many times. There was no turning back."

Teffinger took a long swallow of beer.

It was warmer than he would have wanted but still good.

"That's not of interest to you, though," he said. "What's of interest of you at this point, and to me, is that when I was on the island and Rail's murders were flashing in my mind, there was no murder of Lachey Silk. At first it just struck me as nothing unusual. But the more I thought about it, particularly since Rail even sent me a flash of that Chicago victim, Vampire, I started to wonder if maybe Rail didn't actually kill Lachey Silk. Maybe that's why I didn't get the flash."

"But all the evidence was there," Kovi-Ke said. "The note in the red book on the top shelf, the one that said NOIZ . . ."

"That's what the lawyer Blake told you that Rail told him," Teffinger said.

"True. So what's the issue?"

"The issue is that it the note wasn't put there by Rail," Teffinger said. "I'm about ninety percent positive that Blake killed Lachey Silk. He put the note in the book to set up Rail to take the fall."

"Why?"

"Why'd he kill her?"

"Yes, that."

"I'm not sure," Teffinger said. "The detective in charge of the case had heard a rumor that Lachey was blackmailing someone. In hindsight, I think it was the lawyer, Blake."

"Why? What'd she have on him?"

"I don't know but it must have been big," Teffinger said. "My gut tells me that Blake didn't set this whole thing with you and Nicole Carter in motion because he's a goody-goody guy who wanted to take down a killer without losing his license. He wanted to plant his own murder on someone else. That was his motivation."

"Do you have any proof?"

Teffinger shook his head.

"None, other than the fact that Rail didn't flash the murder into my brain. That's not exactly the kind of thing you can parade out in front of a jury. Like I said, you're the only person in the world who knows what happened that night on the island, outside of me and Janjak."

"Well, maybe you're wrong."

"That's possible," Teffinger said. "That's why I've been keeping close tabs on Blake. It's off the books. I'm doing a lot of it through a private investigator in New York. No one in my department knows I'm doing it. It's not an official investigation. Yesterday I found out two very interesting things."

"Like what?"

"One, Blake's been investigating me over the last two months. He's been doing it through a private detective in town by the name of Anderson Biggs. Two, Blake purchased a roundtrip ticket to Jamaica," he said. "He's landing here at 7:10 tonight and taking off at 10:23 tomorrow morning. It's obvious he's not coming for a vacation."

"He's coming to kill me?"

"Yes."

"Why?"

"Because he's worried that I'm starting to figure out what he really did," Teffinger said. "He's worried that he might eventually get charged in Lachey Silk's death. If that happens, you would be a key witness—the key witness, in fact. You would be able to testify that he told you all about the particulars of Lachey Silk's murder, ostensibly because Rail told him about them. Now, Rail was in fact in New York the night of that murder. However, Blake is afraid that there might be evidence to show that Rail didn't commit the murder, an alibi at the time of death or something like that. So, at this point, you're the biggest piece of evidence against him. I think he's sneaking into Jamaica to remove the specter of that evidence."

"So what do we do?"

"That depends."

"On what?"

"On two things. One, on how mad you are at him for abducting you into that voodoo ritual and then tricking you into a charade. And two, on whether you're willing to be the bait."

She looked at him.

"I'm willing."

"Good," he said. "He's going to come after you tonight. When he does, I'll be there."

"And you'll kill him?"

"He'll leave me no choice."

She held her hand out.

"Shake on it."

He did.

Then he swallowed the rest of his beer, stood up and said, "Let's go. We have logistics to take care of."

61

August 10
Tuesday Night

That night it stormed. Kovi-Ke worked late at the dive shop, catching up on paperwork, dressed in the same clothes she'd worn all day, visible through the edges of the window coverings. At 10:12 p.m., under a dark sky, Stephen Blake snuck silently through the weather to the front door, found it locked, and cut around to the back. That door, luckily, was unlocked. He took a deep breath, tightened his grip on a black eight-inch serrated knife and charged in. Thirty seconds later that same eight-inch knife was embedded in his chest, shoved up to the handle and then twisted twice.

The last thing he saw in the world was Teffinger's eyes.

In the dark, Teffinger and Kovi-Ke got the bloody body into Ugly Tuna 3. They cleaned the shop to perfection and then, under lightning skies, they took a little trip twenty miles out to sea where the ocean bottom was more than a mile deep.

They tied the body to a 35-pound CQR anchor with dozens and dozens of crisscrossed wraps of half-inch rope and dumped it into the black waters.

No one dived there.

No one explored there.

No eyes would ever see the lawyer again.

The fish and crabs would claim the body.

The bones would scatter and eventually get silted over.

Kovi-Ke wrapped her arms around Teffinger and laid her head on his chest. Then she said, "Janjak was watching us. Did you feel her?"

"No."

"I did."

Jim Michael Hansen (sometimes writing as R.J. Jagger) is the author of over 25 hard-edged mystery and suspense thrillers, including the Nick Teffinger thrillers, the Bryson Wilde thrillers, and the Nicole Stone thrillers. In addition to his own books, he also ghostwrites for a popular bestselling author. He is a member of the International Thriller Writers and the Mystery Writers of America.